EDJ OF THE EMPIRE

EMPIRE

Revenant's Omen

Timothy Burns

Books by Timothy Burns

Edj of the Empire: Herrig's World
Edj of the Empire: Revenant's Omen

Look for the next book in the series on January 9th, 2020

Other Sci-fi Books by
Chandra Press

Fusion World: Philanthropy 1 by Joseph Tamone
Shadow of the Demon: Philanthropy 2 by Joseph Tamone
Rijel 12: The Rise of New Australia by King Everett Medlin
Return of Anarchy: The Fall of New Australia by King Everett
Medlin
Thad Saves the Galaxy by C.T. Fleck
Sworld: The Chronicles of Malick by William Harris
Soteria: The Crisis Forge by Roberto Arcoleo
Mirrors: The Shadow Conspiracy by Sonya Duelina Williams
The Moon Hunters by Anya Pavelle
Edj of the Empire: Herrig's World by Timothy Burns

Books by Timothy Burns
Edj of the Empire: Herrig's World
Edj of the Empire: Revenant's Omen
Look for the next book in the series
on January 9th, 2020

Other Sci-fi Books by Chandra Press
Fusion World: Philanthropy 1 by Joseph Tamone
Shadow of the Demon: Philanthropy 2 by Joseph Tamone
Rijel 12: The Rise of New Australia by King Everett Medlin
Return of Anarchy: The Fall of New Australia by King Everett
Medlin Thad Saves the Galaxy by C.T. Fleck
Sworld: The Chronicles of Malick by William Harris
Arachana: The Chronicles of Malick by William Harris
Soteria: The Crisis Forge by Roberto Arcoleo
Mirrors: The Shadow Conspiracy by Sonya Duelina Williams
The Moon Hunters by Anya Pavelle

CONTENTS

DEDICATION

This book is dedicated to readers everywhere, no matter the preferred genre. To those about to read, I salute you.

CHAPTER 1

Villalba, world of a hundred thousand luxurious resorts, where any and every pleasure is for sale. A planet chock-full of tropical island paradises, where the rich come to play and the hopeful come to pray. Fortunes are won and lost here 29 hours a day in the casinos that never close. Gambling for anything, on anything, from cards to shark fights, dice to gladiators; if it can be wagered upon, it's on Villalba.

"If games of chance aren't your addiction of choice, rest assured that whatever is can be found here. We will cater to your every whim. Fantasy fulfillment, pampering, body enhancement, sensory stimulation of every sort - if you can dream it we have a place for you to live it."

And so on ad nauseam. The advertisements have flooded every media outlet in human space for centuries. I'm sure you're as tired of them as I am. *Everyone* has heard of Villalba, and a significant percentage of the population of the empire have made it one of their life goals to visit there at least once. Some want to take in the live shows, others to experience the glamour and luxury, but all hope to strike it rich in one of the many famous low-risk, high-payout games.

Few gamblers ever come out ahead, though. It's a given that the odds are always fixed in the house's favor. That hasn't changed since the first gambling hall opened back at the dawn of History.

Until now. Now, suddenly, if you can believe the rumors, *anyone* can go into any casino on the planet and come away a winner. It's incredibly easy, so the stories go. It's as if the casinos have all decided to generously pay out all the trillions of credits they've collected over the centuries, to anyone and everyone who walks through their doors.

The planet, never lacking for visitors, has now become so popular that, for the first time in its long history, it is now regulating the number of tourists allowed in. More hopeful tourists are arriving in orbit than are being granted clearance to land, and a number of huge passenger liners have taken up permanent orbit to act as highly-over-priced hotels for those seeking access to the easy riches below.

Fortunes are still being won and lost, but now it is the casinos on the short end of the stick, and they aren't liking the reversal at all. For, you see, it is not by their choice that the odds have so drastically changed.

But none of this has anything to do with why I'm here. I am after only one thing: information that will lead me to where the former planetary governor might have fled. Six years ago he ran off with trillions of credits of embezzled money, and more recently he tried to destroy the Imperial capital and everything else in its star system, but these crimes pale beside the one for which I am determined to hunt him down and make him pay: he kidnapped and is torturing into submission an innocent lady friend of mine.

I am the Crown Prince of the Empire of the 99 Stars, and nothing will be allowed to stand between me and my prey. Lumar D'Orneo was already the most wanted criminal in the Empire, but I wasn't on his trail before. I am now, and his days are numbered.

The incredible confusion surrounding the recently implemented traffic control restricting access to Villalba's surface meant nothing to me. I don't often make use of my Imperial credentials to pull rank, but when I do, all official doors are open to me. I asked for, and received, priority landing clearance to the restricted section of the spaceport on Triffin, the island home of the planetary capitol, and an immediate audience with the Imperial Governor.

Olaf Svensson had taken over the planet's top slot when he won the special election that followed D'Orneo's departure six years ago. By all accounts he is a fair, reasonably honest, level-headed man who is doing his best to help the local government recover from the shambles it was reduced to in the aftermath of the arrest of so many corrupt officials of D'Orneo's regime.

I've never met the new governor before, and I was mildly surprised to find him a relatively young man for such a position. He had to be well under a hundred, with a head full of thick blonde hair and big sideburns and mustaches to match. Nor was he a thin man, as so many are these days. Big-boned and meaty, he looked like he would be more at home among his distant Viking ancestors than in the super-luxurious palatial office in which he met me.

An escort of immaculately dressed and spit-polished Marines had met me at the spaceport and conveyed me here, and the razor-sharp major in charge walked with me to the governor's carved walnut office doors. At our approach, the 9-foot tall doors opened of their own accord, and the major stopped just inside, came to picture-perfect attention, and introduced me to the governor using my full name and title before crisply saluting and withdrawing.

I hate pomp and ceremony. It's one of the main reasons I avoid the Crystal Palace back on Alphum and travel among the 99 Stars disguised as a simple cargo freighter. But there are times when I need to be the prince. Plain old Jed Ecnirp would never have been allowed in to see the planetary Governor without having to wade through layer upon layer of petty bureaucrats, which I just didn't have time for.

"Your Highness! Come in and have a seat, please," Governor Svensson said, stepping out from behind his mammoth smokey-grey orion-wood desk and gesturing toward a pair of high backed, ornate chairs sitting near a well-stocked mini bar of gold and polished fornu-heart wood.

The rest of the office was furnished in an equally opulent manner. In several niches in its walls stood obviously expensive abstract sculptures, and off to one side set a round conference table carved from a single great Slyteen mega-pearl with a dozen chairs carved from as many smaller specimens.

He noticed me looking around, and what he said next raised my opinion of him several notches right then and there. "It's all too much for my simple taste, too, Sire. I'd be more comfortable in a plain setting that hadn't cost the government a hundredth as much." The smile on his face actually seemed genuine, too, not the practiced mask of so many politicians. I found myself taking a liking to the man, and I hadn't been in his presence two minutes yet.

No wonder he'd taken the election by such a huge margin over his two competitors.

"Let me guess: this was all D'Orneo's, and some self-important protocol drone is insisting that you have to keep it to suitably impress your most distinguished guests."

He nodded his head. "Exactly right, Sire. I'm glad to see that the talk about your down-to-earth sensibilities is no myth."

"To be honest, I just plain have no use for all the put-on, over-the-top trappings and formalities that so many fools think is a requirement for running the government."

"Then you are a wise man indeed, Sire." He once again gestured toward the bar. "May I offer you any refreshment?"

I took a seat and let him pour us both cups of coffee. After we had sipped and made the appropriate appreciative comments about its quality, he asked about the purpose of my visit.

"I'm hoping to find a clue as to where that scum D'Orneo might go to lick his wounds," I told him. Then, because I was enjoying the company of this rare bird, the honest politician, I gave him a rather detailed account of what had brought me to this point. He sat silent the whole time, politely not interrupting with any questions, and I concluded by saying, "So unless someone calls in with a reliable sighting of him, my best bet is to grill his old cohorts for any hint as to where he might go next."

Olaf, as he insisted I call him, could only shake his head in sympathy. "I would not want to be in his shoes when you catch up to him." Then switching to a more businesslike tone he said, "So how may I help you? The whole of my resources, such as they are, are at your disposal, of course, Sire."

"On my way here I read a summary that said

some three dozen people who'd had close ties to D'Orneo were arrested and are in your prison system. I want each and every one of them located and mind-probed. I presume you have a member of psi-corp on-world who can handle this?"

"I do not know. If you'll give me a moment..." The governor's eyes took on that unfocused, rapidly-moving look of someone accessing an internal computer. In less than a minute he had an answer. "I'm sorry, but no, there aren't any. We did have two, but they were both killed recently. The nearest psi-interrogator is a week away by Naval speedboat. Shall I requisition his services?"

"Yes, at once, and in my name. Damn, I did not want to have to wait that long, but I need every clue they might have buried in their heads."

The delay was a major setback. When I'd checked before leaving Herrig's World, there had indeed been a pair of Psychics here. And, then being what they are, I really hadn't expected to hear of their murders.

"I am truly sorry, Sire. If you would like, I will have my best investigators question these prisoners mercilessly..."

I stopped him with a shake of my head. He knew as well as I that conventional questioning techniques, even those employing tailored drugs and forced regression, cannot withdraw the level of details a skilled psionic can. I hate the very thought of what mind rapers can do to someone's head, but there are times when their abilities are the only way to accomplish what you need.

And the thought of D'Orneo in control of one was enough to frighten anyone, myself included. If frying the minds of all three dozen of his former confederates led to me being able to find him and rescue Melanada, then so be it.

"Well then, is there anything at all that I, or anyone on my staff, can do to aid you, Sire?"

"Not that I can think of, but thanks anyway." I sat back and drank the last swallow of my coffee. It really was a good blend, good to the last drop, even.

A week. 7 standard days, more or less, until the psionic could get here by the fastest military transport. A week more for D'Orneo to torture Mela, to break her mind and her spirit. It had already been over a month since he made off with her. I can only imagine the cruelties he's capable of inflicting on her.

If there was anywhere else I could turn to for a lead on where he might be, I would already be on my way there. As it was, though, these imprisoned former cronies of his were my only potential source of information. And Villalba, being fairly centrally located in relation to most of the Empire, was as good a place to wait as any.

And if I was going to be here for a while, I needed something to keep my mind off Mela's predicament. "So tell me, how is it that two psionics were killed here? I assume it has something to do with whatever's happened to suddenly make Villalba's casinos easy marks."

The pained look that crossed his face, the way his eyes narrowed and mouth drew into a grimace, spoke clearly of how much the planetary disaster had been affecting him lately. "How much do you know about what's going on here?"

He forgot the 'Sire', and I was content not to remind him of it. He suddenly had the look of a man with much bigger problems than a lapse in courtly protocol. "Nothing at all," I told him. "Take it from the beginning."

"It all started about three months ago when a new drug called 'Peek' showed up. Now, this isn't any kind of feel-good or take-me-away drug - we've got plenty of those available legally. No, what Peek does is much, much worse. It gives its user a peek into the future. The way I understand it, the user can see an overlapping image of all the possible outcomes of whatever he concentrates on. The more likely a particular outcome, the clearer he sees it."

He paused there, obviously waiting for me to comment. "Oh yeah, that could play havoc in a casino. How long does this effect last?"

"Anywhere from five to ten minutes in ability, anywhere from a few seconds to a few minutes in precognition." He did not sound happy at all, and I was starting to see why. Even such a short duration was plenty long enough for a user to win a fortune. Despite my concerns for Mela and my need to catch D'Orneo, I was becoming more interested in this problem.

"What form does this Peek come in, and how is it used?"

If it was possible for the governor to look even more distressed, I can't imagine how he would have done so. "It's a powder that can be eaten or drunk in any innocent-looking disguise or snorted directly. So, in other words, people can walk around and do another dose whenever they want."

"Ouch. Are there any side effects? To the user, I mean. The ones to your economy are obvious."

That earned me a wry grin, at least. "Yes, Sire, there are. Apparently it is highly addictive, but whether this is a physical or purely psychological one is unknown, since not all users show the same degree of addiction. Withdrawal seems to bring on extreme agitation mixed with bouts of total confusion. If there are any lasting effects, it is too soon to tell."

"Of course. Any idea how it's made?"

"None. It isn't anything like any natural substance on a molecular level, but at the same time it doesn't appear to be a synthetic molecule, either. It possesses a subatomic structure that is even stranger. It could very well be an entirely new type of matter. We really need more samples to test, but they are hard to come by, as you can imagine. The Dealers see through even our most innocent-looking buyers."

Now it was time for the real question. "So what is being done about it?"

The governor hesitated before replying, whether out of embarrassment at the lack of progress or simply to gather his thoughts, I don't know. At length he said, "I just hope we catch a break soon. Despite the laws requiring payout on every valid wager, more and more casinos are threatening to no longer honor what they call 'suspicious' winnings. Some have started requiring betters to make their wagers 15 minutes ahead, and others have halted all of their instant-win games. I wish I could tell you that we are gaining the upper hand over the suppliers, but I cannot. The truth is, we've made no progress whatsoever in determining where it is coming from or how it is being distributed. The suppliers can literally see us coming. It's extremely frustrating, Your Highness."

That, I could completely understand. The peculiar ability this drug engenders makes it useful to more than just gamblers.

"To be perfectly honest, Sire," he went on, "when I first heard you were here and wanted to see me, I hoped it would be to tell me you'd heard of our plight here and had come to work one of your legendary miraculous planetary cures." A pause, then, "I had no idea that you were in the middle of a personal matter. One in which I completely sympathize with you, for what it's worth."

If that wasn't as transparent a plea as I've ever heard, I'll swim every one of Villalba's third-of-a-million islands non-stop. Well, he *is* a politician, after all.

"Thank you. I do appreciate your help, but I'm going to leave it to you to see that the psi has all the help he needs when he arrives. I'm afraid I'm not very good at waiting patiently, however, so in the meantime I believe I'll keep myself occupied by visiting a casino or three. Who knows, I might get lucky and run into a Peek dealer."

Another hint of a smile crossed the governor's face then, but he quickly erased it. He didn't want to seem too pleased that I had unofficially agreed to investigate.

"I would imagine that's a distinct possibility. From what I hear, they're everywhere."

"And if I do come across one, maybe he'll tell me how I can get into the sales action." I shot Olaf a grin on of my own. "After all, Jed Ecnirp *is* an accomplished smuggler. Not," I hastened to add, "that I'm saying I'll go out of my way, but if I uncover any leads while I'm waiting to hear from you, I'll be sure to pass them on. But I'm sorry, the instant I have a line on D'Orneo I'm gone."

He nodded his head sagely. "Of course, Your Highness. Of course."

CHAPTER 2

When I left the Triffin spaceport the second time I was much more comfortable. Not only had I initiated a sequence of actions which would, hopefully, lead me to Mela, I was also now back in the persona I more and more thought of as the real me. Gone was the expensive custom tailored and flashy jewels worn by the Prince, replaced with the well-made but more pedestrian jeans and dress shirt of a moderately successful freight owner on vacation.

I would have felt even better here wearing my customary weapons belt, but such was prohibited on most of Villalba's islands. But even without blaster or quick staff I was more than capable of defending myself if trouble should come my way. It's just that I prefer the greatest number of options, and I'm more comfortable going armed than not.

But still, it was better to be plain old Jed the

independent freighter than Prince Edj. His Royal Highness might have all official doors open for him, but the kind of people I was now in search of were anything but official. And despite what I told the governor, I had every intention of finding out where this Peek was coming from and putting a stop to it. It was wrecking a whole planet's economy and dealing with situations like that is what I do.

There are no true continents on this ocean world, just upwards of seven hundred thousand islands. And since the planet has no appreciable axial tilt and is situated at almost a perfect 90-degree angle to its yellowish-orange sun, the vast majority of these would be considered tropical isles on any other world. And a shallow, salty ocean and no moons or seasons mean no tides or storms to disturb the peaceful tranquility of the hundred thousand resorts built upon them.

No *natural* storms, at any rate.

Yet sometimes man can outdo nature herself, especially when motivated by an emotion as strong as thwarted greed. Witness what happened to the *Golden Shark.*

I had decided to begin my research in one of the many lower-end casinos, of the type favored by the rougher working-class crowd. Situated on an island mostly given to high-density housing and support infrastructure for the employees of the classier resorts, the *Golden Shark* struck me as a prime candidate for Peek dealers.

The management must have thought so, too, and had instituted drastic measures to thwart both dealers and users. No eating or drinking was allowed anywhere on the premises anymore, with the exception of one bar, and customers leaving there were not allowed to enter the gaming areas for 30 minutes afterward. The selection of games have been seriously curtailed as well. No computerized, single-player machines were operational; no slots, no video poker, no holo dicott. Closed, too, we're all the games based on the roll of dice or other randomizers, so no craps or roulette tables were left.

The casino still had to entice customers to risk - and hopefully still lose - their money, though. Closing its doors was not an option; it *had* to keep making a profit. So what was left fell into two categories: wagering on remotely viewed events like fights and races, and strictly supervised card games.

The first was fairly safe, from the house's perspective. Like every other casino on the planet, the *Golden Shark* had taken to requiring all bets on the outcome of such events to be registered well in advance of their termination. Peek could not help anyone there.

But even though there were many competitions of one sort or another being conducted all over the world at all times, and anyone could bet on them from nearly any casino, they still only appealed to a certain percentage of the gambling public. Many more people insisted on only risking their money on something that they had - or at least *felt* like they had - some influence on the outcome of. If any casino shut down its card tables, it might as well not bother being open.

So the management of the *Shark* had adopted the policy of keenly observing every player. If anyone touched their mouth or nose they were immediately ejected from the premises, their winnings forfeit. No one was allowed to play until they had been watched for at least 15 minutes. The size of their bets was carefully controlled, as well. Progressive stakes were no longer allowed to accumulate, nor were side bets allowed anymore. All these rules were legal, and they were posted on large signs all over the floor.

What was not so clearly defined was what constituted 'suspicious behavior'. The patrons were warned that this would get them kicked out and their winnings confiscated, but it was apparently up to the pit bosses and security personnel to decide what this involved.

I was seated in one of the many 'waiting galleries', watching the gaming from afar while waiting for my mandatory quarantine time to expire, when this policy backfired on the management in the worst way.

There were approximately 120 gamblers in a gaming area that was designed for five times that many, and maybe 30 security staff backed by innumerable AI-monitored cameras watching them all. In the short time I'd been in the casino - no more than ⅔ of an hour - I'd already seen three gamblers get ejected for various alleged rule infractions. They weren't happy about it, but they all quit protesting when enough toughs surrounded them.

The fourth one was a mizkra of a different smell, as they say.

It started with a large bio-augmented man who was a local labor leader of some sort. I'd been watching him off and on with idle curiosity, for he was attended by several hangers-on, and in my experience it often pays to keep a weather eye on someone like that. He was playing Blackjack, and on average was winning a little more than he was losing. He was following all the casino's rules, of course, and after a bit, he started to bet the maximum allowed almost every time.

Some hands he lost, but most he won. The more he won, the more spectators drifted over to watch his winning streak, the way they will in gaming parlors everywhere. And he was on fire, too. He won hand after hand, with no apparent violation of the rules. He wasn't eating or drinking, nor did he ever raise his hands anywhere close to his face. In fact, the more he won the stiller he sat, moving only as much as needed to, as if all too aware that any action at all could be considered suspicious and cost him his accumulated winnings.

Until, apparently, merely continuing to win

was considered suspicious.

With no warning, half a dozen burly bouncers closed in on him from all directions. All conversation and movement around him stopped, and I could clearly hear one of the security men say, in the bored monotone of someone who has said the same words time and again, "In accordance with the *Golden Shark's* anti-cheating policy, your actions have been deemed illegal and you are hereby commanded to leave the premises immediately."

The tough wasn't halfway through his rehearsed spiel when the gambler rose and turned to face him, his face going red and fists clenching. As soon as the bouncer finished, the gambler - whose name I later learned was Jerry Johns and was therefore called 'JJ', erupted in a violent denial. "I done no such thing! All my winnings is legal and I ain't going nowhere!"

The bouncer didn't look so bored anymore. JJ was big, and he was angry. "Sir, you can either leave peacefully or I will use force to remove you."

JJ was fenced in by 6 big security toughs, but he didn't look the least bit concerned. "I said I ain't going! Now get out of my face!"

They stood there staring at each other, neither one moving yet, when one of JJ's friends outside the ring of toughs said, "He said he ain't going. You'd best just leave him be if you don't want a whole lot of trouble."

Another one spoke up from the other side. "These new rules suck! An honest man can't even win anymore!"

I don't know if it was planned or not, but by this point several more started protesting. Shouts about how the casino was stealing player's money competed with demands that other games be reopened. More people added their voices to the growing confusion, and then suddenly words were replaced by battle cries in the sounds of a frustrated mob giving in it to built-up grievances.

Furniture and gaming tables were smashed, along with quite a few heads. The riot gained momentum from there, as more and more disgruntled - or perhaps violence-craving - people came in from outside. Before it was over the entire interior had been gutted, every piece of equipment smashed.

Most of the original security staff escaped early on, recognizing a hopeless situation when they saw one. Only three were killed, including the one who had originally confronted JJ. He'd had his carbon-fiber-reinforced neck snapped, and not a single surveillance camera saw who did it. Some dozen more earned mementos of varying degrees of severity, but in general, made it out in one piece.

Among the rioters were a number of injuries, some fairly severe, but no fatalities. Most of these occurred not during the trashing of the casino itself but were inflicted by the police that had been called in to break things up.

As for myself, once I saw which way the wind

was blowing I made for the exit and watched the proceedings from a safe distance. I don't mind mixing it up in a good cause, but this wasn't my fight. I did learn one thing, though: the situation on the planet, in general, was growing worse by the day. Things could not keep going like they were - something was going to have to give. The *Golden Shark* was the first casino riot, but it wouldn't be the last.

My next attempt to find some Peek met with more success. After a quick trip back to my ship to upgrade my wardrobe to something more suggestive of a very successful merchant, I chose a more respectable casino, and I looked not on the gaming floor but in the bar. I had realized that every word said in the casino proper was sure to be recorded and monitored.

Now, I know my way around a bar. It's not that I'm a heavy drinker - I'm not. I even have an implant that can cleanse most drugs from my system as fast as I ingest them if I desire to keep a clear head while blending in with certain types. It's just that, in the course of doing my job, it's often there that I go to find information or make contact with those I need something from.

And having been around as much as I have, I know who to talk to in any bar to find anything I might need, whether it be the down and dirty on someone, a hot weapon, or anything else. In this case, one glance around told me that I'd find what I was after in one of the classy call-girls who were working the crowd.

"Buy me a drink?" asked the one who slid into the bar stool next to me. She was a looker, of course, a raven-haired siren in a low-cut sequined body sheath dress that hugged her perfect body like a second skin. Cosmetic enhancements of all sorts are a justifiable business expense in her line of work, and unless she had been lucky enough to be born with exceptionally perfect genes, she'd spent her fair share with the body docs.

I gave her an admiring glance and said, "Sure thing."

She waved to the bartender, who promptly slid an overpriced concoction before her. After taking a tiny sip of it she leaned in very close and said, and a soft purr right into my ear, "You look like a guy who knows how to show a lady a good time."

"And you look like a lady who deserves to be shown a good time," I said with my patented to Don Juan smile. "Would you care to join me in the casino for a bit of gaming? I find I always do better with a beautiful girl by my side."

She shot me a put-on pout, her full lower lip protruding almost comically. "I wish I could, but the mean old bosses have declared that escorts are no longer allowed on the gaming floor. So why don't you stay here with me for a bit? I love to dance. By the way, my name's Candi."

I shrugged my shoulders noncommittally, casting a disapproving glance at the crowded dance floor.

"I'm John." I touched my glass to hers. "Pleased to meet you."

We both drink, then she said from even closer than before, "Are you sure you don't need anything else to help you do better?"

Time to play innocent, or at least not too knowledgeable. "I thought there was no way to, you know, get lucky at the tables anymore."

Her smile told me I'd come to the right place. "There are ways, and there are ways." She looked around at the fairly crowded bar and few unoccupied tables. "But perhaps we should go somewhere more intimate to talk."

As I led her to one of the only empty booths, Sam told me something very interesting. ((Several people here, including your new companion, are carrying small amounts of something that exists partially outside of your standard time dimension.))

(Great work, pal. It's got to be Peek. Hmm, how far away from it can you, uh, 'smell' the stuff?) I sometimes run into problems describing some of Sam's peculiar senses, but he usually knows what I mean even if I don't.

((In the quantities present here, only from a few dozen yards. It has a cumulative effect upon the underlying fabric of space-time, however, such that I suspect the more there is in one location the farther away from it I will be able to detect it.))

Oh, better and better. Sam was my very own

personal Peek detector.

Candi saw me smiling as she slid in beside me, and I let her think it was because of the way her hand slid along the top of my thigh. "We don't have to dance if you don't want. There are encounter rooms here if you just want to slip off for a bit," she purred suggestively.

"How about if I come back and find you after I make good in the casino?"

She saw then that I seemed to be more interested in money than her charms. Her hand withdrew, and her voice took on a more businesslike tone. "Have you ever done Peek before?"

I could honestly tell her that I hadn't. "But I've heard enough to know what to expect. What I don't know is how to do it now that all these new rules are messing everything up."

Her smile this time had a definite touch of guile in it. "There are ways. I can teach you how, and set you up with five hits, for, oh, let's say 1000 credits."

Now, I'm no genius, but even I could tell that she was trying to gouge me deep and that it was my own fault. I had, after all, pretty much come out and told her that she'd never see me again once I left here. Still, I couldn't let her think I was that easy a mark.

"What, 200 a pop?" I shook my head. "That's awful steep. Why, my... friend... said it was going for half that when he was here."

"Inflation, baby. Supply and demand and all

that. And don't forget, you're buying more: I'm the only one who can tell you how to get away with using it."

"750. That's 150 each," I counter-offered.

"Nuh-uh. 150 is what it goes for flat rate. You can give me that plus another 150 for my knowledge, or good luck trying to get it on your own."

A master negotiator she isn't, but I smiled at her anyway and nodded. "Okay, I suppose that's fair enough."

"Wait right here, then. I need to visit the powder room."

She returned a couple of minutes later, and when she slid in beside me this time she took my hand and pressed a small, soft object into it. At the same time, her implanted computer established a body-field link with mine and asked me to authorize the payment, which I did.

"Put that in your mouth, and bite down hard the first time you want it. After that, use a softer bite. And don't try to double-take it. It won't do any good. You have to wait until the first one wears off to take the next hit." She smiled again, her predatory one this time. "And come look me up later. Ask the bartender if you don't see me."

I promised I would, but we both knew I wouldn't.

CHAPTER 3

N eedless to say, I didn't try my luck at the casino that night. Instead, I took my purchase and let the most sophisticated scanner on the planet have a look at it.

This incredibly sophisticated device, ansible linked to classified databases on several different planets, was not located in Villalba's planetary forensics laboratory. Nor did it belong to any of the elite security services that maintained offices there. It was, rather, aboard my highly customized tramp freighter, the *Wah*, an integral part of the automatic system, actually.

What I learned confirmed what both Gov. Svensson and Sam had told me about it, mainly that it is like nothing else ever seen in this universe. In fact, according to both Sam and my equipment, parts of it exist in several additional dimensions that modern physicists can't even agree on the properties of.

And every resource I referenced agreed that it

could not have been made in this universe.

I know what you're thinking: isn't this universe *the* universe, the one and only? Well, you would be both right and wrong. To us here on the inside, the universe is everything. You can never fly a ship past its borders, for there are no borders. However, this set of dimensions we inhabit are just a few out of uncountable trillions. Other combinations open up into different universes. In some of these, things may be similar, like you might have length and height and something that reaches in another direction that isn't width. And something could be created there that, if somehow brought into our universe - our set of dimensions - would have existence in both.

Or something like that. That's the gist of what I got from the physicist back on Alphum who Mike insulted, anyway. Stuff like that is so far above my head that all I can do is look at them and say, "If you say so."

What it boils down to, though, is that there were no precursor ingredients that could be tracked down. And yet I really, really needed to know just where the stuff is coming from. Sure, Peek is overturning Villalba's economy and costing the Imperial Treasury lost revenue in the form of the taxes the casinos must pay on their profits. But even beyond that, I have to think of the military potential. If an enemy force got hold of it, no defenders would stand a chance.

Obviously there is a lot of it being made and

used, and it had to come from somewhere. The question was, was there one source or many?

How was I going to find out? That was the next question. Once I realized the greater danger Peek poses, any thoughts of a slow approach went out the airlock. For a normal drug, the standard police procedure of either infiltrating the distribution network by undercover agents or forcing lower-level dealers to give up their suppliers might work, but they take a lot longer than I was comfortable giving it.

What I needed was a straight line right to the top. One way to gain almost instant access to the highest levels of Peek production came to me right away, but it is one that I loathe to employ, for it would involve aligning myself - and thus the Crystal Throne - with some of the most reviled beings in the galaxy. I spent the rest of that evening trying to come up with any other way to break into the racket. I even considered taking a stealth flyer and buzzing every island while Sam sniffed for a big stash, but eventually decided that would probably be a waste of time.

By morning I had come to the conclusion that, as much as I didn't want to, I was going to have to pose as a Revenant.

There are probably people on the far side of the galaxy who have never heard of our Ghouls. To them, I say ignorance truly is bliss. The rest of us hold them both in morbid revulsion and mortal fear. This is because they are that quasi-religious cult that believes in gaining immortality through replacing worn-out or inferior body parts with ones taken from living people. Rumored to be spread throughout our own Perseus galactic arm, they're most active in and around the metals-rich Birmingham globular cluster that is home to my Empire and our nearest neighbors. Culture-grown organs are anathema to them, as are synthetics of any sort. They hold that a person's life force only grows in natural bodies, and by transplanting organs and body parts they can harvest that mysterious energy and make use of it themselves.

This would be bad enough even if it were all there was to them, but in reality they are much worse, for they claim that this *vitae* weakens over time, so they are always searching for new 'donors'. And they are very lax in seeking consent from their suppliers, if you know what I mean.

Anyone who has any dealings with them - and there are a surprising number - can become indebted to them very easily. Merely telling one 'thank you' implies that you acknowledge their claim upon you, in their minds. Likewise, they're quick to latch onto any other minor social convention and twist it into presumed indebtedness. And once they consider someone in their debt, that person has only to wait until the time comes that their payment is due. On that day, only flesh will suffice.

So why, you may ask, do so many people choose to deal with them instead of doing the sensible thing and running away as fast and as far as possible? Well, not everyone in this galaxy is as sensible as that. Some are able to convince themselves that they can partake of the riches that associating with the Revenants can bring them without eventually falling prey to those same masters. For the Ghouls, you see, are the cluster's acknowledged masters of the interstellar drug trade. They are the ones who can move vast quantities of illegal substances from star to star with impunity, for there are very few who would risk angering them by searching their ships.

Anywhere a Revenant goes he is treated with the utmost courtesy and respect, for again, no one wants to curry their disfavor. And woe upon anyone who tries to overpower one, because that is a sure way to volunteer to donate all of one's flesh to the Order of the Eternals. They are neither forgiving nor easy to defeat. A lot of people swear there's something truly magical about them, for each individual is protected by a mystical, supposedly vitae-derived shield that, while undetectable by any sensor, protects them from any attack, whether physical or energy based. How this is accomplished is a secret closely guarded by them, of course.

It is by this that they are known, for a Revenant may have any physical appearance. Some are indistinguishable from ordinary humans, while others revel in the grotesqueness of their patchwork nature, but all project an aura of supreme confidence and invulnerability.

Of course, there are some few people in the galaxy who may think to impersonate one for some reason or another; perhaps to intimidate others or to gain the advantage in business dealings. These imposters, however, are few and far between, for two reasons. One is that true Revenants do not hesitate to demonstrate their immunity to weapons of any sort, and the other is that, if a fake lives long enough, the real Revenants will find him and claim his body parts for themselves.

So now you can hopefully understand why I tried to come up with any other way to reach the peak of the Peek pyramid without having to go through the Revenants. I, alone among the trillions of people in the galaxy, can successfully impersonate one without risk of either death or dismemberment, for they are aware of Sam's existence. Not only that, they know that they can do nothing to me without bringing the wrath of the Emperor himself down upon their whole Order.

To do so, however, I would have to offer the true Revenants a concession for not disowning me, and it is that which I was so hesitant to do. With my flesh denied to them, what else might they claim in payment?

I was fairly confident that the Revenants were not already involved in Peek marketing, for the simple fact that there were no hints of it on the other worlds; and it is an Interstellar transport that they rule, not low-level distribution on any one planet. So theoretically I should be able to present myself as a representative of their Order and be taken straight to the highest level here on Villalba, but to do so I would have to first contact the real Revenants and inform them who I am and what I'm doing.

But this, of course, runs the very real risk of giving them the entire galactic Peek market if I'm unable to permanently shut down production. If they do not yet know about Peek, they will once I contact them.

I wish I could peek not 15 minutes into the future but a month or so. Then I would know whether my all-or-nothing gamble would pay off. But alas, such knowledge is denied to man. The best I can do is forge ahead blindly, trusting to my wit and skill.

With one phone call, I wagered the very existence of the Empire itself against my belief that Peek has only one source and that I would be able to contain or destroy it.

My crown had never felt heavier.

Another phone call, this one to Gov. Svensson, furnished me with the name and location of a mid-level Peek dealer, courtesy of an informant the police were putting the squeeze on. I wasn't thrilled to be starting so low, since I didn't think a Revenant coming in would be so lacking in information on the higher-ups, but at least I wasn't starting from street-level guys or casino-bar gals.

I planned my attire for this evening very carefully. In accordance with what was known of Revenant beliefs, everything I wore had to be made out of natural materials, so a shopping trip was in order. By the time I set out, I was sporting a shimmery black-blue feru-silk shirt complete with long sleeves and a ruffled front tucked into a pair of skin-tight elp-hide trousers of a natural cream color and wearing genuine Earth sharkskin boots. The outfit cost a small fortune, but I guess that was half the point. Revenants are extremely wealthy and are famous for indulging in all sorts of sensual delights.

At least I had my own jewelry to wear, in the form of a woven gold and diamond strand necklace and a pair of rings set with stones worth a small starship. What I did not wear were any electronics or other high-tech devices, nor any weapons. Revenants have no desire for the former and no need for the latter. The only exception they make is their scalpels. Every Revenant carries one, usually openly. These they use to extract and stasis-hold flesh from their victims while healing the wound sites. As none have ever been secured for examination by Imp. Intelligence, their exact technology and working is unknown. I'd fabbed mine based on descriptions, which was okay since I'd never use it anyway. Looking like an ornate belt dagger straight out of a medieval renaissance fair, I wore it openly on my belt in a jewel-studded sheath.

The governor had been able to provide me with the phone number for this Peek dealer, a man who hadn't been brought down yet because the police were watching him in the hopes that he would lead them to bigger fish. They had no idea just how much bigger a whopper I was going to catch through him.

I made the call from a public vid-comm booth at the Triffin spaceport, which would be natural enough given my role. The man who answered was a small, almost dainty fellow of late middle age, whose sharp, pointy features were nearly hidden by a wild mop of unruly brown hair hanging down in his face in the fashion of a man a hundred years younger. He was seated on a balcony overlooking a wide bay, the ocean far below as calm as a sheet of glass.

"Who are you and how did you get this number?" was his less-than-cordial greeting.

I gave him a tolerant, patient smile that I knew he would soon take to be anything but. "I am the Eternal Aloysius of the order of the Eternals, Mr. Malloy."

His Adam's apple bobbed as he swallowed, and he sat upright in his chair to look straight into his camera. He obviously recognized the Order. "Excuse me, Eternal. What can I do for you?"

"I have a matter I wish to discuss with you, sir.

His eyes, the one that I could see, anyway, darted from side to side as if looking for a way out but finding no openings. "Of course. Anything

I can... I mean, um, what can I..."

It was amusing watching him squirm, but I knew better than to let it go on too long. "In person," I said sharply.

"Oh, certainly. Where would you like to meet?" He swallowed again, obviously far beyond nervous.

"That looks like a splendid panorama behind you. Where are you located?"

He gave me his address, and my neuroware told me it was on a mountainous island about two hours flight away.

"Excellent. The journey will allow me to take in more of the beauty of this extraordinary planet. I shall see you in just over an hour."

His eyes - I could see both of them now, he had rushed his hair aside - went wide. He knew where I was calling from. I could see him wondering how I was going to get to him so quickly.

"I'll be awaiting your arrival, Excellency."

'Dreading' it was probably closer to the truth, but I didn't correct him. Without another word I shut off the comm and hurried to the rented luxury flyer I had already secured and had waiting.

Once aboard, I gave it Mr. Malloy's address as well as an Imperial security code which allowed it to override the air traffic regulations that limited its speed to subsonic velocities. Revenants consider themselves beyond the need to obey the laws of mortals, and if my act was to be believed I had to play my role to the hilt. If people complained about the sonic boom my flight caused, it would only serve to further reinforce my disguise in the eyes of those Peek lords I was after.

Mr. Malloy was still on his balcony when I arrived, I saw, as I instructed my flyer to park in a hover even with the top of its railing. He had an even half-dozen augmented toughs with him, and four of them aimed blasters at me as I lightly hopped down to the deck.

I slowly shook my head, an amused expression on my face. "Is this any sort of welcome for one of my stature?" I sighed loudly, showing the guards not a bit of concerne as I looked directly at Malloy. "Very well, let's get the formalities out of the way. Allow your men to shoot at me, then dismiss them. What I have to say is for your ears only."

Four blaster bolts, fired from almost point-blank range, would be enough to make even a man encased in high-grade battle armor with active force fields just a tad bit nervous. Yet I, standing there in nothing but my all-natural clothes, didn't bat an eye. Sam, whose existence is only loosely anchored to the moment we call the present, clearly saw the order in which the four guards would fire and where their blasts were going. It was the simplest thing for him to interpose himself between each of these and me at exactly the right time to absorb them.

No one saw any of that, though. Unless he chooses to reveal himself, Sam is invisible and undetectable to any sensor based in our dimension, so all they saw was their shots simply failing to have any effect on me whatsoever. I didn't even look at the men who had just tried to kill me. Instead, I casually strolled over to the seat beside the one Malloy had risen from and, with a gesture towards that, asked, "May I?"

Now that my host knew for certain that he was dealing with a Revenant, his face lost all its color and his voice had a quaver in it he couldn't entirely conceal. "Certainly, please do. May I offer you a drink or... or anything?"

He remained standing as I sat down. He was wringing his hands in nervousness and shifting his weight from one foot to the other. Seeing him so flustered like that, I couldn't resist tightening the screw a notch. He was, after all, a man who made his living exploiting the weaknesses of others.

"Why are you so fidgety, sir? Does my presence fill you with such terror that you cannot engage in a civilized discussion?"

His Adam's apple was at it again. It took him several swallows to frame a reply that he thought acceptable. "No, sir. I'm just surprised that you chose to honor me with a visit." he took his seat and made a visible effort to calm himself.

"I make you uneasy. For this I apologize, and we'll come right to the point. I desire for you to arrange a meeting between myself and whoever controls the production of this remarkable substance known as Peek. You can do this, no?"

I could all but see him thinking just by watching his face. A tangible feeling of relief swept over him, visible as a relaxation of the hard lines around his eyes and loosening of his tightly drawn lips, as he realized that he was not going to be required to enter into any long-term contract with the Order and that he would most likely keep all his body parts. Swiftly following on the heels of that, however, and evidenced by a widening of his eyes and a catch in his breathing, was the realization that he had no idea who the ultimate source of Peek was.

If I had been being myself then, I probably would have backed off when I saw that and given him the chance to pass me on up a few levels to someone in a better position to lead me to my ultimate goal. But no true Revenant would ever show such compassion. They tolerate nothing less than perfect performance from everyone under them, and everyone to whom they spoke was considered to be under their authority.

"You seem to be at a loss for words, sir. May I suggest that your answer to me be that you can indeed accommodate my simple request?"

Only a slight tremble showed as he nodded his head. "Yes, of course, your Eternalness. Excuse me, I need to make a call or two."

I smiled at him. "Certainly." I then got up and ambled to the balcony rail, where I gazed out and down to the beach far below, hands clasped casually behind my back.

When he realized I wasn't going to board my

flyer but intended to wait right there for him to make his calls, he cleared his throat and said timidly, "Sir? It may take some time to make the necessary arrangements. Perhaps you would care to visit one of our renowned casinos in the meantime. As my guest, of course."

Ever so slowly I turned around. I'm not the least bit sadistic; I don't derive any enjoyment from causing or witnessing discomfort in anyone. Nonetheless, the pure terror on Mr. Malloy's face as he thought he displeased me in some way almost made me laugh. Perhaps I was just really getting into the role I was playing, but I had a momentary impulse to really mess with him.

I didn't indulge my dark side, though. That's a slick slide for anyone to slip onto, and for someone with my power it is well-nigh unforgivable.

Still, I had to stay in character. "Business before pleasure. It is a rule you would you do well to learn. Go into your home and make your calls. Tell your superiors that the Eternal Aloysius will meet with them at a place of their choosing this evening at the latest. Stress to them that anyone who keeps me waiting incurs a debt for my time. *Go*."

He couldn't get inside soon enough. I estimated that a mid-level man in his position would have to go through at least three higher-ups to get words to the very top. At each level he would have to convince them that he was in earnest, which could take several minutes. My guess was that it would take somewhere between 10 and 20 minutes for him to have an answer for me, but perhaps I underestimated the desperation engendered from a visit by a revenant, for he returned after only eight.

His long, unruly hair was brushed to either side of his face, so I could clearly see the look of relief on it as he announced, "Good news, sir. Mr. Pablo Guzman will see you at your convenience. You are invited to join him at his residence or suggest another location should you prefer. He asks only that you relay your preference so that he may make suitable arrangements."

I rewarded Malloy's quick work with another smile. "You see, that wasn't so hard. You may inform Mr. Guzman that I accept his invitation and will see him promptly at four of the clock at his home. And for your service, I shall make it known to my brethren how well you aided me. You can be assured that, should there come a time when your assistance is again required, we will not hesitate to call upon you. Until then, live long and prosper."

I shouldn't have left him so terrified, but I just couldn't help it. With any luck he would pack up and run for a backwater world and never have anything to do with the drug trade again.

CHAPTER 4

I didn't have to ask Mr. Malloy for Pablo Guzman's address because as soon as he said the name my neuroware queried the police database and found that, sure enough, he was well-known to the local authorities.

A 56-year old native of the world Nuevo Catalonia, he rose through the ranks of that planet's criminal organization without ever once being convicted of any crimes until, at the age of 29, he was implicated in the suspicious death of a rival. No charges were ever filed against him, but shortly after this incident he immigrated to Villalba. He avoided drawing any legal attention to himself for the next decade or so, but eventually, his name began to be whispered as a man not to be taken lightly.

Investigators here have Guzman pegged as a major player in the illegal fantasy fulfillment market. Most of the services and consumables he provides are legal, but it is suspected that he is the go-to man for anything desired that other brokers in the market either can't or won't supply. None of the latter category has ever been successfully traced back to him, however, so he has the official status of 'under observation'.

While this might sound like he is being watched and all his electronic communications intercepted, what it really means on a world that attracts so many millions of visitors every year is that, unless he really goes out of his way to attract law enforcement attention, he is a nobody.

But his days as a legal 'nobody' might well be coming to an end now that I have him in my sights.

There are a lot of very rich people who have homes on Villalba, so I can't say that Guzman's villa was one of the largest or grandest such residences. If it were almost anywhere else, though, it would have ranked right up there as one of the nicest in the world. Set high atop a sheer drop to the placid sea, it crowned one of the innumerable mountainous plateaus that were the favored building sites for the planet's wealthy, giving it a view of both forest and ocean. Native pink marble blocks have been exquisitely carved in bas-relief to depict a wide variety of floral and geometric patterns, and these faced every wall of a Roman-style house that surrounded an open courtyard.

I brought my flyer down on the grass in the central courtyard at precisely one minute before four o'clock and stepped out just as the hour changed. A Revenant is always true to his word, down to the smallest detail.

As I looked over my reception committee, Sam informed me that there were several large concentrations of Peek present, of two different types. The new variety was much crisper and cleaner, he said, struggling for appropriate adjectives. It also, he said, gave off a distinct extra-dimensional emanation that it should be possible to detect with the right kind of specific sensors. I filed this information away for later, suppressing any outward sign of my pleasure at learning that.

Three richly-attired men stood in front of an ornate, multi-tiered fountain adorned with statues of nude nymphs and satyrs. I recognize the one in the center from file photos as Guzman. Dusky skin, tall and muscular, with thick black hair worn short and neatly cut and huge, drooping mustaches, he was dressed in an all-white suit right down to his white shoes. The only color to his outfit was the corner of a red handkerchief that was neatly folded and precisely tucked into the left breast pocket of his unbuttoned jacket.

To his left stood a short man who was not more than 4 1/2 feet tall and very nearly as broad, whose pale skin and vein-encrusted bulging muscles identified him as a native of the high-gravity world Thulis as much as his distinctive fringed leather sleeveless tunic and trousers did. And on Guzman's other side, wearing a hooded crimson robe belted with a wide thread-of-gold band, stood a woman whose entire left side, from crown to foot, was revealed by my infrared sight to be cybernetic.

"Welcome to my home," Guzman said with an expansive gesture, both hands held high and wide. "Please, come and join us, Eternal Aloysius." His right arm swept around to indicate a quintet of chairs set in a circle under the overhang of a second-story walkway, near an area filled with weight-lifting gear.

I joined them by the fountain, none having moved from there yet. "Who are your associates, Mr. Guzman?"

"Ah, forgive me, sir. This gentleman here is Mr. Mino Jorn, and the lovely lady is Mistress Stephanie Swone. They are my two closest business associates, as you correctly surmised. Now come, let us retire to the shade."

We all took seats then, the others allowing Guzman and I the ones that placed our backs to the wall.

"I understand you have a matter of some urgency to discuss with us," Jorn said, his voice a deep bass rumble. "But may we offer you any refreshment first, a cold drink or snack?"

That didn't surprise me at all. Thulisians have an incredibly high metabolic rate and are constantly needing to fuel their massive musculature, so for them, no meeting can be conducted without food. And if I was being myself, either Jed the trader or Edj the Crown Prince, I would have accepted his offer as a matter of course. But as

Aloysius, I had already expressed a desire to not waste any time.

"No, that will not be necessary. I am here, as I am sure you suspect, to discuss the drug Peek. Tell me, Mr. Guzman, how did you come to know of this remarkable substance?"

Guzman nodded his head. "About four months ago an... underling approached me with a tale I at first took to be pure fantasy, telling how he had discovered a magical substance that allows one a peek into the future. I was skeptical, of course, but the truth of it was easily verified. I immediately saw the advantages this could give a person where games of chance are concerned and undertook to become the exclusive distributor of it."

"I see," I told him, keeping my voice and expressions carefully neutral. "And what is to keep someone else from reverse-engineering a sample and setting up their own manufacturing and distribution network?"

Guzman's face broadened into a toothy smile. "Ah, that's the beauty of Peek, you see. It is totally unlike any other substance in the universe at the most fundamental level. I don't understand all the technical details, but it is apparently composed of extra-dimensional material that only comes through into our universe at one specific location. So it cannot be reproduced or counterfeited, no matter how badly anyone might want to."

My expression didn't change, but inwardly I was smiling from ear to ear. He couldn't have given me better news. A single source meant no worries about anyone else popping up with more once I shut this one supply down.

"That is quite a coup for you, a substance as valuable as this that you control the only possible supply of. The profit potential is truly astronomical. I can't help but notice, however, that the local authorities are doing their best to make it impossible for your customers to profit from using it."

"That is, unfortunately, true", Guzman said when I paused a moment.

I gave him an opportunity to go on, but he seemed reluctant to broach the subject that they all assumed I was there to discuss. When he said nothing more, I gave them a wry grin and said, "Oh, come now. We all know why I am here. There are many more uses for your commodity than merely bilking a casino, and a whole galaxy full of potential customers. To be quite frank with you, we of the Order of the Eternals are surprised you haven't made any advances to us yet. And you *would* contact us if you had any intentions of transporting Peek to other worlds, would you not?"

The expressions on both Guzman and Jorn's faces became clouded with concern. I thought it was over the threat implicit it in my last words, but as it turned out, I was completely off the mark in my interpretation.

"As a matter of fact," the Kingpin said, "the

thought had occurred to me. It turns out, though, that has one very serious drawback. You see, it won't work anywhere but here in this star system. Try to take it elsewhere and it simply ceases to exist. My scientists tell me this is somehow due to its extra-dimensional origin." He held his hands above his lap, palms up. "So what's a guy to do? I know the market for it here is drying up; all I can do is milk it as long as I can while I look for other ways to turn a profit."

It actually made a certain amount of sense to me. If part of Peek's structure were somehow linked extra-dimensionally to its source, it might well have a maximum limit to the distance it can be separated from that source, whatever that might be. And if true, my worries about its military potential were groundless. I felt as if a great weight had suddenly been removed from my shoulders.

That feeling lasted only brief seconds, however, before I felt an even greater weight begin pressing down on me, quite literally. It was as if I were being subjected to a very rapid, uncompensated acceleration in a defective spacecraft.

Or as if someone had activated a localized-gravity coil concealed under the floor.

Too late, I realized that Jorn and I were seated closest to the workout area. The Thulisian grinned as Guzman and Swone got up and took several steps back. As they did, the gravity increased even more, to the point where I felt like I weighed ten times normal. My chair back reclined of its own accord, stopping at about a 45-degree angle, and I was pressed into it so hard that even my bio-augmented muscles couldn't so much as raise a finger. I was trapped.

Trapped, and on the verge of losing consciousness as my lungs labored to draw breath into my too-heavy chest and my heart struggled to pump oxygen-rich blood up the incline to my head. If it weren't for the ultra-efficient oxygen-carrying artificial respirocytes in my bloodstream, I'm sure I would have died there.

But as long as the gravity didn't increase anymore, I knew I would survive. (Be ready to knock out the grav coil, but don't do it unless it gets any higher,) I told Sam. I wanted to let my captors think they had me at their mercy. People tend to talk in situations like that, and I had a lot of questions for them.

"And to answer your other question," Guzman went on conversationally, "we did contact the Revenants. You have no idea how much I had hoped they would come up with a way to transport Peek out-system, but it is just not to be. Mino, don't just stand there. Search him."

Even the genetically-modified heavy-worlder seemed to be moving slowly and carefully, which told me that the gravity was higher than he was used to. Hopefully, that meant it was as high as it would go. If so, I would be fine, because my systems were already compensating. I could breathe easier and no longer felt on the verge of passing out.

"One good thing did come about from my association with the body snatchers, however," Guzman said, a gleam lighting up his eyes. "They told me just now that you are not one of them. I don't know how you pulled off the blaster-proof routine earlier, but I will. Keep looking, Mino. He can't have that strong a shield generator implanted. Remove his shoes and clothing."

My shirt was cut off of me, and my shoes followed.

He turned to the robed woman, who had not said a single word yet. "Mistress, what is the Order saying about our guest?"

When she spoke, her voice sounded oddly flat and even, obviously a product of her cybernetic side which she chose not to tune to sound more human. "They are most *interested* in inspecting this imposter. We can expect their arrival momentarily."

Oh stars, did I miscalculate. I thought that since there were no reports of Peek on other planets, that meant the Revenants just hadn't heard of it yet and, by extension, that there weren't any presently on-world. I didn't even stop to consider that there might be Eternals here already on other business. And my pact with their Coordinating Council, who were so eager to extract a promise for a future Imperial boon in return for allowing me to impersonate one of them, would probably not be honored by the ones here before the deal was struck. That's just the way they operate.

And even though I wasn't too worried about ending up like Mistress Swone, it would probably not be a good idea to be here when they arrived. Oh well. Even if I didn't get everything I hoped for, I'd still learned a lot and felt a lot better about the whole Peek situation now. It was time to go before the big dwarf got any more intimate with his search.

(Okay, Sam, nix the gravity and give me a lift out to sea.)

I felt the oppressively-heavy weight remove itself from me for a too-brief moment, but before I could draw so much as a single unlabored breath it was back in full force. This was not what I expected, to say the least. (What's wrong, Sam?)

((A backup generator kicked in once I disabled the power. I will now destroy the minz coil.))

Again the gravity returns to normal, but this was accompanied by the activation of a stasis field which held me completely immobile. And unlike when that beast D'Orneo held me in his force field, this one was not tuned to allow me to so much as breathe. It was as if I was instantly encased in solid stone.

If Sam couldn't free me, I was going to die. Even with my artificial red blood cells ability to transpire gases through my skin in an emergency, there would soon be no oxygen left in the unmoving layer of air surrounding me. Once their 10-minute internal supply ran out, it would be curtains for me.

Thoughts of all I had left and done filled my mind, foremost among them to worry that I might not live to rescue Melanada from D'Orneo's evil clutches.

And through this, I still heard something that made me even more determined to fight. It was Guzman's voice saying, "You cannot fight some-one who can see the future."

CHAPTER 5

Why wasn't Sam doing anything about the force fields? (What's going on? Get me out of here.)

I have never, no matter how seemingly dire the circumstances, heard Sam's mental voice sound as worried as it did when he said, ((I am trying, Sire, but I cannot locate any active field emitters.))

Talk about disconcerting. Sam is supposed to be able to put out any fire I could get myself into. What was wrong with him? A force field doesn't just pop up out of nowhere. There has to be a source somewhere. (Well, look harder. I can't even breathe.)

((I still detect no energy fields. Perhaps your paralysis is a result of something else.))

Oh, great. Now he wanted to argue with me. (I don't care! Just get me out of here!)

The next things I felt were at once hard to describe and very simple. Sam, using his incredible ability to manipulate gravitation, let just enough of the space-time warping of his stupendously dense quantum singularity bleed through into our universe to counteract the pull generated by the mass of the planet below me. Since he did this from a spot above me and towards the open courtyard, I began to rise at an angle, aiming towards open sky.

Now, if I could be towed around like that, it should mean there was no force field on me. The fact that I was still being held in a stone-like embrace thoroughly confused me. What was not the least bit confusing, though, was the incredible pain that shot through my body the instant I started moving. It was as if I were somehow anchored to that very spot on the planet's surface, and every atom of my being was resisting being moved from there with an ordinate stubbornness.

(Stop! Don't move me!)

My mental cry came before my conscious mind had even thought things through, as if my subconscious knew exactly what was causing the agony and how to put an end to it. Even before my blessed pain limiting tech could kick in, Sam did as I commanded and halted. As soon as his pull ceased, so did the terrific pain. And almost as an afterthought, so too did my ability to draw breath return. I still could not move so much as an eyeball, but my lungs were once again sucking in the sweet elixir of life.

"Do not attempt to leave us and you may continue to breathe," Guzman advised me. "I may not know yet how you work your tricks, but that doesn't keep me from countering them before you even try. I suggest you simply wait patiently the arrival of our Revenant friends."

That was *not* high on my list of most favorably anticipated events, let me tell you. My agreement with their Coordinating Council would mean nothing unless I could convince these Revenants that I had such unheard-of protection, and there was no guarantee I would even be allowed to plead my case to them.

I had to figure out what was holding me and escape it, and soon.

((Are you unharmed, Sire?))

(As long as you don't move me, apparently. Are you sure you can't see *any* energy restraints holding me?)

((Quite sure. May I suggest that you are being held not by technology but it's psionic means?))

Of course. Sam can detect any form of radiation or natural force, so for him to say there was nothing unusual affecting me meant there really wasn't. And what did that leave? The one force both he and I were powerless to resist: that of the mind.

So the next question became: who was the psionic? I don't think there was any doubt in my mind who that was. Someone that powerful would never be content to take second place to anyone else. Guzman's own history spoke of a man constantly forging ahead in his chosen field, regardless of who or what stood in his way. It had to be him.

But how to defeat a psionic on Peek, who could actually see the future? I was trying to work that out when the situation suddenly got an order of magnitude more complicated. The true Revenants arrived.

A small, nondescript flyer landed in the courtyard beside my rented luxury model, and some small part of my mind realized another mistake I had made. Instead of flaunting their great wealth and power, as I had thought they would, they apparently subscribe to the philosophy of attracting as little as overt attention as possible. Too late, I saw the wisdom of this. They are, after all, smugglers and thieves of the most horrible sort.

"Welcome, welcome to my humble abode," I heard Guzman saying enthusiastically. He and the others were not in my line of sight, and I still could not move so much as my eyes, but my ears were unimpaired. "I'm so happy to see you again."

Yep, he had to be the psionic. Only someone as wrong in the head as one of them could honestly welcome the arrival of Revenants.

It would be easy for me to have Sam swallow Guzman, but unlike my bodyguard, I prefer to find non-lethal ways of dealing with my opponents. That's a good habit for a Prince or Emperor to be in, I'd been told.

(Okay, Sam, I need you to do your flashbang routine right in front of Guzman's face. Make it enough to stun him but don't cause any permanent damage. And as soon as he's out of it, fly me away as we planned before.)

A black hole is one of the most awesomely powerful things in the multiverse. Unrestrained, one can absorb entire galactic clusters and make itself felt across distances of billions of light-years, like the one known as the Great Attractor is doing. That one is drawing in galaxies from all over the universe and will most likely consume every bit of matter in our dimension eventually.

Sam is nowhere as massive as that, at least as far as anyone knew. What makes him different is that the interplay of energies that surround his singularity are so complex that a sentient mind arose within them, and with this came the ability for him to shunt all or some of his forces into other dimensions. But at need, he can precisely control how much, and of what type, of energy he allows to leak back into our reality.

If he wants to, he can filter a fraction of the Hawking radiation that arises as energy is sucked into his event horizon into visible light. He can also allow some of the air around him - if he is in an atmosphere, of course - to be sucked in, and if he does this for just a fraction of a second it produces a fantastic rush of wind and a thunderous booming. In fact, he can precisely simulate the light and noise of a lightning strike if he's moving fast enough when he does this.

Having this occur so close to someone's face is

a surefire way of momentarily distracting them, as I've used to good effect many times in the past.

Unless that person can see into the future.

I couldn't close my eyes in preparation, but I didn't need to - they may look natural, but my peepers are high-tech replacements, capable of much more than nature's model allowed for. One advantage among the many this gives me is that I can recover from abrupt changes in lighting levels almost instantly. This means that bright flashes don't leave me temporarily blinded. As I've said before, being the prince has its advantages. I'm built to survive.

Another bonus of having eyes like mine is that my peripheral vision is as clear as my direct line of sight. This is how I was able to see Guzman, who had just stepped into the corner of my visual field, suddenly turn away and cover his face with his hands an instant before Sam made like an aural/visual stun grenade.

And since Guzman wasn't stunned by it, his mental hold on me wasn't disrupted. When Sam again went to fly me away, the incredible pain struck me full force again, too.

I must have lost consciousness this time, for the next thing I knew Guzman was standing over me and the side of my face with stinging as I'd just been slapped.

At least I was still breathing.

"I warned you against trying anything." He shook his head slowly, like a father admonishing and misbehaving child. "Whatever you try, I'll be ready for it. I think it is time you answered a few questions."

The paralytic hold over me relaxed as far as my head and throat were concerned. Not only could I lick my dry lips, I could turn my head and get my first to look at the Revenants. There were two of them, a man and a woman. The man was a truly grotesque Frankenstein's monster looking amalgamation of mismatched parts taken from at least a couple of dozen victims. He wore a sleeveless tunic and loose pants that did nothing to conceal the myriad differences in skin coloration and muscular development of limbs that each had parts from several 'donors.' His hairless head was misshapen, the top half of his skull noticeably larger than the bottom, and his eyes were of two different colors as well. On his leather belt rode his scalpel, and he was adorned with enough jewelry to make a video diva jealous.

As hideous as he was, his companion was, in her own way, even worse. The right side of her body - what was visible under her toga-like gown, anyway - was made up of several different sources, but she had at least made some effort to choose similar skin tones and body sizes. What made her strike me as a true monster was her left side. From skull to toe, all the skin was the same and bronze tone and every part was perfectly proportioned to every other. It was obvious that it had not been pieced together, for there weren't the slightest traces of scarring or discontinuities anywhere. It would have been easy to think that this was her natural body except for one thing: it looked exactly like a mirror image of the organic right half of Mistress Stephanie Swone.

They saw me looking at them and both grinned. The man said, "Behold your future, imposter". His voice fit his appearance, being deep and gravelly.

"I think not, for I am the one your Coordinators agreed to allow to pose as one of you." I had to try.

The woman laughed. She had gotten Stone's voicebox, apparently. "What an amusing tale! Marek, have you ever heard such arrogance?"

Marek shook his lopsided head. "Never, my dear. And I've seen a lot of donors try and talk their way out of their commitment." His finger tapped his scalpel in a slow, steady heartbeat while he looked me over like a butcher inspecting a fresh meat animal, trying to decide where to make the first cut.

"He is, of course, all yours," Guzman said, "but I would like to know how he's performed his tricks. I would consider that a fair exchange for my capturing and holding him for you."

"What 'tricks' are these?" The female Revenant asked.

"Well, Mistress Twilla, it's like this.." he told them how I'd ended up there. While he was doing that, I was busy trying to decide what my next move should be.

Obviously, I needed to get away from Guzman and his blasted psionic control. I could still have Sam remove him completely, but that would be my last resort. What else, then? Allow the Revenants to take me away and then escape from them? Possible, I suppose, if they didn't start chopping me up right away.

No, too risky. What I needed was a situation where Guzman's prescience wouldn't help him. Hmm... maybe I was going about it backward. If what I needed was to put some distance between the two of us, and I couldn't go anywhere, but what did that leave?

Another slap brought me back to the present. "Don't drift off now," Guzman said sharply. "You have some tech that I want. You also have some flesh that my friends want, and they will have it one way or another. The question is, how much pain will you be put through and what shape will you be in afterward, huh? That depends on how long you hold out before telling me what I want to know."

He was holding a wicked-looking knife in one hand and a manual saw in the other and looked like he would thoroughly enjoy using them on me.

I wasn't going to give him the chance to. (Sam, take Guzman for a swim. Drop him a good distance offshore.)

The drug lord must have seen what was coming, for he started to scream even as he was whisked over the villa and down to the sea far below.

I expected my paralysis to end then, with his removal and him having his own survival to concentrate on, so I was more than a little surprised when nothing changed. The pain didn't return, but neither could I move. I couldn't even blink or speak. Only my lungs worked.

Could I have been wrong about who the psionic was?

Marek's laughter was as rough as his gravelly speech. "I don't think he wants to answer you, Guzman." He looked at Jorn and Swone, who were standing a little way back. "If you master returns, tell him that we thank him for his gift."

With that, he picked me up and carried me to their vehicle. I still couldn't move.

CHAPTER 6

Once I was deposited on a bench seat and the hatch closed behind us, all my paralysis went away and I was overcome with a feeling of pins and needles all over my body as muscles that had been held immobile were finally allowed to move.

Before I could even sit up, Twilla had her hand behind me to help. "You are safe now, Your Highness."

"You knew?" I asked.

"You didn't want us to blow your cover, did you?" Marek replied reasonably.

"No, of course not. Thank you."

"Where would you like us to take you?"

I looked down at my bare chest. "How about to my ship at the Triffin spaceport?"

Marek went forward to give the flier the destination, and Twilla took a seat across from me. "Did you find out all you needed?"

"No, as a matter of fact, I didn't. Why did you

have to give me up to that psionic Guzman in the first place?"

Her smile, spread across two sets of lips, with more than a little creepy. "That dense grazmich is no psionic. He is, however, quite ruthless and conniving. If he thought he'd captured a true member of the Order, it would be just a matter of time before he tried it again. That we could not allow."

I nodded in agreement. "I suppose not. But if he's not psychic, how did he... Wait. I wasn't released until you got me in here, yet it came over me before you arrived." I looked at her, thinking. "You and Swone?"

She nodded, holding up her left hand and admiring it. "When we need to replace a brain, we do it one hemisphere at a time. That way, the dominant personality can impress itself upon the new neural structure. When Miss Swone came to be indebted to me, I was pleased to discover that her unique talent for telekinesis was not diminished by the removal of half of her brain."

That was going to give me nightmares at some point, but I deliberately put it out of my mind for the moment. I had other things to concentrate on just then. "Don't tell me any more, please. I don't need to hear it."

Marek chuckled from up front.

"Instead, why don't you tell me what you know about where the Peek is coming from since you blew my shot at getting that from Guzman?"

"If I gave you that information, that would

place you in my debt, would it not?" Twilla asked with a grin. "Above and beyond that what you owe to our Coordinating Council, that is."

I should have seen that one coming. Revenants *never* give anything away for nothing. Already I owed their Order a favor, to be called in at their leisure. I can only wonder what the true cost might be for that one. Could I justify doubling it?

"Oh, the worry that is writ large upon your Royal brow! What could such as I want from you, you are wondering?" Twilla laughed. "I almost wish I did know the source of this substance, for to place you in my hand. Sweet would it be, the agony in your breast of waiting for my price to be named."

She was playing with me! They had no more clue as to where Peek came from than I did.

I shot her a grin. "Who needs you, anyhow? I just happen to have a mobile Peek detector in my orbit anyway! You know, extra-dimensional to extra-dimensional and all that."

She looked at me sideways. "Then why did you need to make like one of us in the first place?"

"Because at the time I decided to put the Crystal Throne in hock to you I was worried about Peek getting into the hands of a military force. I thought I couldn't afford the time it would take to sniff out its source. Shoot, I didn't even know then that it only *has* one source."

"So is that what you will do now?" asked Marek, in his grating growl. "Nose around every island until your friend gets a hit?"

"Well, that was my first thought, but now I think I know a way to get a broader overview, shall we say."

Both Eternals seemed to realize I was going to say nothing more about my plans than that, for it was their nature to give nothing away. The rest of the flight we talked about nothing of importance, and I was careful to avoid any verbal traps where I might have ended up in their debt.

As Marek set the small flyer down beside my ship, Twilla tried one last time to get me. "Marek and I will be here on Villalba for several more days. If you find yourself at a loss and wish us to question anyone for you, all you have to do is ask. It would be our pleasure to come to the aid of the Empire."

I gave her a smile over my shoulder on my way out the door. "I'm sure it would, but you know I cannot condone your methods. Goodbye."

As I entered my ship and donned fresh clothing - my customary loose pants and semi-formal shirt - I consider doing exactly what Twilla had offered to do on my behalf; namely, going back and forcing a location out of Guzman and not taking 'no' for an answer. While that was certainly still an option, it also carried with it the very likely possibility of alerting whoever was in charge of Peek production to my presence and thus driving them into deeper hiding.

No, my plan of tracking down the supra-universal source by means of scanning for the emissions of what I was thinking of as Mega Peek still sounded to me like the best bet. The only problem was, I had no idea how to go about rigging a sensor capable of detecting it.

It took me all that evening and most of the next day, working via ansible with some of the brightest minds in the Empire, and with frequent consultations with Sam about specific properties of the compound, to come up with a detector that should be able to spot it. And even after all that, the effective range on this new sensor was calculated to be, at best, on the order of several hundred miles.

The problem was that, because of the diffuse nature of the extradimensional component of the Peek, neither Sam nor the technological detectors could pinpoint its exact location. In fact, from up too close it just seemed to be everywhere.

Still, that was a drastic improvement over Sam's own personal detection range, which topped out at less than a single mile under the best circumstances. And even better, this device was something that could be duplicated and distributed to security forces the world over.

By the morning of my fourth day on Villalba, police everywhere we're scanning for concentrations of Mega Peek. They were under strict orders to take no action whatsoever other than to report any hits to the governor's office. I did not want anyone to run and hide before I had the opportunity to check them out in person.

Within hours of the detector's deployment, the entire planet had been scanned and three different locations had been tagged as containing significant quantities of the good stuff. One was Guzman's villa which, while it was possible that it housed the trans-dimensional source of Peek, I dismissed as the least likely.

Of the other two, one was on one of the inhospitable equatorial islands and the other underwater several hundred yards away from there. These places were known to be part of a private fantasy-fulfillment resort owned, via a series of intermediaries, by Pablo Guzman, which said to me that they were prime suspects for what I was after.

Orbital surveillance showed there to be an underground complex on the barren, sunscorched island, connected via tunnels to the undersea domes.

Such facilities were not unheard-of on Villalba, I learned. With the planet having almost no orbital tilt, its equatorial regions maintain temperatures year-round well in excess of what all but the hardiest plants could tolerate. Humans found it impossible to live out in the open, but technology will triumph over nature whenever there is sufficient desire. And with habitable land being at such a premium, some developers found it financially justifiable to build both under the surface of the ocean and in the cool interior of otherwise unusable islands.

'Dreams Alive', as the complex was called, was basically a huge movie set where a combination of force fields and holograms were used to simulate any setting the customer might want, while gravity and atmospheric modifiers completed the illusion of being on any planet. An industrial-sized nano-assembler provided appropriate props and accessories, and a staff of expert roboticists was on hand to customize the more animate background characters.

All of this existed for one purpose: to enable the guests to live out any fantasy they could imagine. Some wanted to experience hunting the ceramic-armored wildlife of Herrig's World or engage in other such highly dangerous pursuits, while other customers chose to use the facilities to recreate long-lost locales or events. There were limits to what could be done even in such a well-equipped arena, though, especially when it came to things like acting out violent tendencies against other sentients or engaging in certain other illegal activities. This is where Guzman was alleged to make all things possible, although only for clients who were both trusted to maintain secrecy and able to pay the exorbitant premiums he demanded.

Clients of this sort had certain requirements of their own, of course, including confidentiality and security. For this reason, the resort maintained a small but very competent security force, and it is the presence of this that made me choose to approach it the way I did.

Posing as a guest was not an option since openings were booked months in advance and massive preparation was needed for each one. But since going in with a full-scale assault squad would only make the on-site security feel threatened and could easily lead to unnecessary bloodshed, I chose the middle ground.

All commercial properties on Villalba are subject to periodic unannounced inspections by the planet's tourist safety board, so posing as such an agent would not only give me official entry, it would not unduly spook the locals. After all, everyone knows that such inspections are mere formalities and the inspectors aren't actually there to stir up any trouble.

Obtaining the necessary identification was simply a matter of informing the governor that I needed it. By the time I had changed into a suitably impressive outfit of military fatigues, combat boots and my ever-welcome quick-staff, I had an official badge and data card that proclaimed me to be Inspector First Class Connor Paxton.

Gov. Svensson didn't like my idea of going in alone. Of course, to the best of his knowledge I *was* alone, so I can't say as I blame him for his concern. To make him feel better, I agreed to allow him to place a squad of Imperial Marines on alert and have them waiting in low geostationary orbit where they would not alarm anyone at Dreams

Alive yet be able to do a tactical insertion and reach the complex within minutes if needed. I didn't think I'd need them, but the governor was a nice guy and I didn't want to hurt his feelings by refusing.

Besides, I wasn't on Peek so I couldn't know for certain whether their presence would be vital or not, and it doesn't hurt to cover all your bets.

For transport I requisitioned a government flyer from the capitol's motor pool and arrived above the seemingly deserted island shortly after local noon. Transmission of my inspector's ID code gained me immediate access to the complex's landing field, an enclosed cavern kept separate from the scorching outside air by huge force fields across its open mouth.

When I stepped out of the nondescript flyer I was met by a sharply-dressed young man in a crimson and gold-braid uniform who insisted on escorting me directly to the manager's office. As we went, I couldn't help but notice that everything about the resort screamed money, from the thick, rich carpeting to the wood-paneled walls and crystal-and-brass old-fashioned light fixtures. The clientele here was obviously used to being surrounded by the finer things in life.

Down a short corridor from the reception foyer was the office of Floyd Pritchard, to whom I was introduced by my escort before he closed the wooden door on his way out. "Good afternoon, Inspector. Welcome to Dreams Alive, the finest fantasy-fulfillment resort in the Empire."

A tall, gaunt man with sharp, ax-like features who wore a pointed goatee and well-trimmed mustache below loosely curled black hair, Prichard was dressed in an expensive charcoal-gray suit adorned with diamond cufflinks and heavy multi-jeweled rings. Every bit of this I read as a uniform he wore to announce to both guests and employees alike his wealth and importance.

He rose from behind his paper-cluttered desk to greet me, although he made no effort to shake my hand. To him, I was just another functionary whose presence had to be accepted but who was in no way his equal. "It is an unexpected honor to host an inspector of your rank. I trust that you will find everything in order here."

There was no hiding his nervousness. He was unable to stand still, his bony hands fidgeting and his eyes darting everywhere but to my face.

"Relax, Mr. Prichard. I'm not here to cause any disruptions. Far from it, in fact. You see, I am of the old school. I've been with the TSB much longer than our current governor has been in office." I gave him a knowing look, confirming his unspoken question.

"Things were certainly different under Lord D'Orneo, weren't they?" he gestured me towards the lone chair in front of his desk as he reclaimed his seat, much more comfortable now that he thought he knew what I wanted.

I sat down and leaned back. "That they were.

It's a shame there aren't more men like you and I left, who remember the old ways."

His smile told me I had read him right. According to the information about the resort the governor's office had provided me, Pritchard had only come into his position after the fall of D'Orneo's regime. He would have been aware of the massive corruption at the highest levels of both government and business but not in on the biggest money floating around, not like his former boss who had gone down with so many others in the massive cleansing that took place after.

"In fact," I went on, " it is because of this lack of respect for the old ways that has taken hold of men's hearts that I have come to you."

Oh, I most certainly had his attention by this time. He was laid back in a relaxed posture, but his former restlessness had transformed itself into a fixed obsession on every word I spoke.

"You see, I recently learned that certain others in my department suspect this very resort of being the source of the entire planet's supply of Peek."

Prichard's eyes widened and his jaw dropped. "Don't bother to deny it. I have my own impeccable sources of information," I told him flatly. I could see that he was on the edge of panic, only my insinuation that I was less than incorruptible giving him a shred of Hope to hold onto. He started to open his mouth, then closed it.

"No, I'm not here to bust you. Anything but.

You see, not everyone views Peek as a problem. I'm here to see what can be done to protect the supply line."

The resort manager let out an audible sigh of relief. "That... that is most welcome news, inspector. I am certain my superiors will be very glad to hear it as well. As I am certain you are aware, I am but a mere steward entrusted with overseeing a limited part of the total operation, though, so any question of policy will have to be referred upward."

"I understand," I said with a nod. "My purpose here today is more in the nature of familiarization. Now you know there's a problem and that a potential solution exists. What is left for you and I is to determine how best to protect what you are charged with protecting. Only after I know what will be required to ensure this will I know how much to charge Mr. Guzman for my services."

The look of relief on his face as I mentioned Guzman's name told me that he was buying my story 100%. After all, I *must* be legitimate if I knew the secret of the ultimate head honcho's identity. And if I already knew that and hadn't busted *him*, anything he revealed to me was merely incidental from here on out.

"Of course," said a very relieved Prichard. "What can I do to help?"

CHAPTER 7

What I learned from Mr. Pritchard was very, very interesting. He confirmed that Peek was indeed being processed and packaged for distribution in a secret part of the offshore section of the resort. That, in and of itself, was nothing new. What he told me next, though, was worth every bit of what I had gone through up to this point.

Raw Peek was delivered to the undersea portion of the complex in a submersible spacecraft roughly once a week. And the next delivery was due in mere hours.

Bingo!

A lifetime's practice in controlling my facial expression kept me from giving away the elation I felt, but inside I was all but jumping for joy. Even while I sat at Pritchard's office half listening to the self-important little man go on about how much faith and trust Guzman placed in him, I was already planning how I intended to take advantage of what I just learned.

Using a ship capable of both submerged and space operation for deliveries was actually a very shrewd idea. Such a hybrid craft is very rare, so anyone attempting to follow it would almost certainly run out of luck when it entered or left the ocean. And while it is absurdly easy to remotely track an atmospheric or space flight, all that changes once it drops below the waves. The delivery ship could make planetfall literally anywhere and travel as a submarine for any distance. It was brilliant, actually.

There was one flaw in the otherwise ideal plan, however. They hadn't counted on me being on the trail and my determination to track them down.

Nor did they know about Sam's unique talents.

Among his myriad of other matchless talents, my friend and guardian is possessed of an innate ability to sense gravitational fluctuations to a degree only dreamed about by the designers of military and scientific sensors. It has to do with his multidimensional nature, so I've been told. I don't really understand it, but he can feel the variations in a planet's gravity caused by the mass of a single vessel passing between him and it.

All I would need to do was wait above the resort and be ready to follow the delivery ship. Unlike anyone else on the planet, I could remotely track it until it emerged from the sea. After that, it would be merely a matter of using conventional traffic-control assets to follow it back to its destination, which would presumably be the ultimate source of the world's most recent ills.

Pritchard was still going on about how valuable he could be to me, but I cut him off by pretending to receive a call on my implanted comm. Sure it's an old and dirty trick, but it still works. I made my excuses to him and was soon back in my borrowed government flyer. Before much longer I was aboard my own ship and had taken up a hover high in the stratosphere directly above the Dreams Alive complex.

I had worried about missing the Peek delivery in the time it took me to get into position, but after more than two hours of watchful waiting those fears were suddenly put to rest.

((Sire, I detect a submerged vessel with a density high enough to be a spacecraft approaching the target location,)) Sam suddenly announced, much to my relief.

To him, the difference between a spacefaring vehicle and a planetary one of any type is perfectly clear, since he can feel the presence of the high-density core of a standard reactionless space drive. I knew better than to question his identification.

As much as I wanted to capture and question the crew of that starship, I thought it wiser to allow them to depart unmolested. With no psi-corp interrogators available there was no telling how long it might take to wrest the location of the Peek source from their no-doubt deceptive and duplicitous minds. No, simply following them would surely be both simpler and quicker.

Yeah, right. I should have known better. Any plan that simple and foolproof is just waiting for the right fool to come along, and in this instance I ended up wearing the jester's cap. I was so sure that the fact they were using a submersible space-craft meant that at some point they would head for space. Sounds like a no-brainer, right? So where did Sam actually track the submarine to after almost a full day's journey? The edge of the tiny southern ice cap.

"Are you *sure* you can't find it?" I asked Sam, for about the dozenth time. And for as many times, he patiently replied that he could not.

((I am sorry, Sire.)) he added this time. ((But the mass of the ice is preventing me from detecting anything else. Perhaps if we were in a vessel suitable for undersea travel I could sense the Peek itself.))

I can't say I hadn't suspected something like this, not after so many long hours of watching the submarine head steadily southward. I guess I was still convinced that they would eventually surface and head for space. That's the only reason I can come up with for not calling the governor and having a military submersible join the hunt.

Not that it would have done any good, as I came to find out. Sure, there are plenty of submarines in the water-world's seas, but there are no armed warships at all on or under the peaceful pleasure planet's ocean. The best I could do was arrange for a search-and-rescue sub to be flown in to the edge of the ice cap, a procedure that cost me a couple more hours.

At least I was able to feel fairly confident that the Peek delivery ship didn't escape while I awaited this S&R vessel's arrival, for it turned out that the entire southern ice cap is only a few thousand miles in diameter and is entirely surrounded by a ring of very sensitive sonic listening buoys. These had been deployed to enable oceanographers to track the migration of schools of large whale-like native fishes, but they worked equally well for detecting the passage of a submarine.

Or they did after the governor ordered the research institute that owned and maintained them to turn over their data, anyway.

Unfortunately, all they could do was tell us that a vessel had indeed gone under the ice just about when and where Sam had said. And we were lucky to get even that much confirmation, they said, because the ship we were tracking was so silent It could only be heard from a relatively short distance away from any individual sensor. This worried me until the same scientists assured us most confidently that, despite this, they would be absolutely certain that they would know if our target emerged, for their coverage of the ice's perimeter was complete and redundant.

Since Sam could not watch the whole area himself I had no choice but to take their word for it. I normally wouldn't have so trustingly accepted such an absolute claim, but in this case I learned that the man in charge of the sensor ring was a retired Imperial Marine, a colonel with several decades experience doing precisely this type of work. Civilians I don't have the greatest faith in, but career military men are a different matter. As Prince and heir to the Empire, I know just how good most of our dedicated military personnel are.

The same went for the captain of the S&R vessel that finally arrived. Another ex-marine, Capt. Thos Panoss had come to Villalba and started his own private undersea rescue company shortly after his discharge from active service, as I learned from a quick web search on him. He greeted me with a crisp salute when I jump-packed from my hovering ship to the deck of his vessel, the *Mercy Mia.*

The ship itself was a streamlined cylinder reminiscent of nearly every other submarine ever built, some 100-odd feet in length and painted a bright orange. It was capable of atmospheric flight as well as underwater service, and I wish I had called for it much sooner. Its upper deck was flat, and as it gently bobbed on the surface of the calm sea the captain and several others stood at attention as I flew down in my combat armor.

As I returned his salute, my practiced eye gave the captain the once-over. He stood tall and proud. Even so, he couldn't be more than a couple of inches over 5 feet tall. His solid build and military bearing more than made up for his lack of height, though, and he projected an air of supreme self-confidence that came through in his every word and gesture. I estimated his age to be somewhere not too far north of a mid-century and he was dressed, like his crew, in a simple, practical uniform of dark blue cargo pants and short-sleeve gray pullover shirt devoid of any decoration or insignia save that the captain's shirt had a gold collar. The taller man standing beside him wore a silver collar while the other three's shirts were unadorned.

"Welcome aboard the *Mercy Mia*, Your Highness," Capt. Panoss said formally. He then introduced his first mate, Georg Kiata, and of the three crewmen, whose names I promptly forgot. "We are honored to be of service in any way we can. And as I understand it, your mission is somewhat urgent, so might I suggest we proceed to the bridge and get underway promptly?"

I liked him already and let him know it by my smile as I removed my suit's helmet. After we dropped into the interior of the sub via a section of deck that turned out to be an elevator platform, I was led to the small vessel's command-and-control center. This was a long, narrow compartment filled with more readouts and controls than I thought a battleship would need, much less a sub.

When the first mate saw me looking over the bewildering array manned by a lone crewman, he chuckled and said, "Don't worry, Sire. Nearly everything is run by the computer, as it should be. These are all merely manual backups, and we only use them during contingency drills."

I grinned back at him and nodded in understanding. "Of course. My own ship is the same way. I just didn't realize that controlling a sub required so many stations."

"A submarine is actually more complicated than a spacecraft," the captain told me. "And one like this that can also fly in atmosphere at supersonic speeds *and* carries a full suite of location and rescue equipment, well..."

"I fully understand, Captain. And it's that location gear that I have particular need of at the moment."

"Yes, Sire" he replied, snapping back into professional mode. He pointed toward one of several unoccupied control stations along the bulkhead. "This is the main sensor station. If you would be so good as to transmit your search criteria to it, we can begin the hunt."

My internal computer did indeed contain a full set of every bit of identifying information I had been able to compile concerning the sub-ship I was after, and as soon as I zapped it into the S&R sub's systems that computer put all of the vessel's resources to work searching for any trace of the target.

I was fully aware of how unlikely we were to find the Peek source simply by searching an ever-widening cone from where the other sub had gone under the ice, though. The rescue sub's sensors had not been designed to pick up on the extradimensional signature that was my best bet for tracking it down.

Fortunately, I had one of my Peek detectors with me. "There is one more input I would like to incorporate into your vessels and systems, Captain." I briefly told him what I wanted and why, and he himself took the detector from me and went to mount it near the bow of his ship and tie it into the sub's network.

He returned a few minutes later, and after a couple more spent working on one of the computers, told me that the new sensor was integrated into his systems and seemed to be working. "I suppose we won't know for sure until we actually get a hit, though," he said at last.

"In the meantime," he continued, "may I offer you some lunch, Your Highness? I'm afraid we don't have a chef on board, but I did recently have a FoodWizard model 3580 installed, and it makes some mighty fine grub. Well, better than the old model 2200, anyway."

I had to laugh. "You had a 2200 and your crew didn't mutiny? I'm impressed."

"Why do you think we now have the 3580, Sire?" The mate asked with a chuckle. "The mutiny was narrowly averted by our captain's wise decision to upgrade."

Lunch was not as bad as the two officers would

have anyone believe. They were both full of apologies for the mediocre quality of the fare, but I assured them - in all honesty - that I've lived on far worse at times.

The rest of the afternoon and early evening I spent immersed in the ghostly realm that was painted by the sensors of our undersea, ice-capped environment. I am used to deep space, where distances are measured in thousands or millions of miles and things are just as clear at astronomical distances as they are up close. The dampening, distorting effects of the water all around us, that made details of objects mere miles or less away fade almost into imperceptibility, was a new and somewhat unwelcome additional strain on my already strained perceptions.

After more than a full day spent following and then searching for the elusive prey, I was profoundly relieved when the Peek detector at last registered that oh-so-welcome trace that meant the chase was finally at an end.

And what a strong return the detector picked up. Once we started drawing closer, the reported concentration just kept going up and up. Soon even Sam commented on it, despite our being still several miles from its source.

"Alright, Captain," I told the sub's commander as he stood beside me watching the sensor panel, "this is where I get out and go it alone."

"But, Sire..."

"No buts, Captain. You are not a military vessel

and I am heading into a potentially very hostile situation. I'll not endanger you and your crew."

"With all due respect, Sire, my crew and I place ourselves in danger on every mission. And while the *Mercy Mia* is not an Imperial Naval craft, we are far from defenseless. In fact, I would venture so far as to say that we are safer here than in any but the most advanced combat subs. In addition to the enhanced detection gear necessary for some S&R jobs, we are also equipped with ridiculously-over-powered adaptive shielding."

I was actually impressed by the man's earnestness. He seemed to be quite willing to commit his entire crew to engage an unknown but undoubtedly well-defended enemy, and his ship did indeed have more going for it than I had expected. Still, things would surely be better all-around if I could sneak up to the still-mysterious facility or whatever it was that lay somewhere ahead of us in the crushing stygian depths."

"Be that as it may, Captain, I am still going on alone. I don't want to take any chance of alerting those I am after of my presence, and I can travel much quieter on my own than your sub can."

His look of confusion was quite understandable. As far as he knew, there was no method of long-distance underwater propulsion that I could employ that could not be heard from miles away. I forestalled the protest I could sense coming by saying, "I have more resources at my disposal than are apparent."

Capt. Panoss chuckled. "Of that I have no doubt, Sire. Some of your exploits are legendary. However, before you totally dismiss my offer, I feel I should make you aware of the full capabilities of my sub. You see, I am something of a tinkerer. I have significantly enhanced several of the systems aboard over the years, and in two cases have created what are, to the best of my knowledge, completely unique systems. One is a force-field based method of digging through seafloor silt."

He shot me a wry smile. "I know, not very relevant. The other, though, you might be interested in. One of the greatest dangers to undersea operations here on Villalba comes from the so-called giant spider-kraken. This is a huge, tentacled creature that evolved to prey on the largest fish, some of which are larger than the *Mercy Mia*. It ensnares its victim in a high-strength web that it uses to drag the animal down to crushing depths. This beast has very highly sensitive hearing, and any noises whatsoever absolutely infuriate it. So to be able to come to the aid of any vessels it has immobilized in its web, I had to come up with a noise canceling system that makes us totally silent on the water."

"In short, Sire, you are aboard the quietest submarine in the Empire. I can take you to the front door of whatever is down there and I guarantee you they'll never hear us coming."

TIMOTHY BURNS

"How the blankety-blank did they manage to build *that* with nobody noticing?" asked an incredulous 2nd Mate Kiata. His sentiment was shared by all of us on the cramped bridge, which was actually everyone aboard but the two men on duty in the engine room.

As to what had us all clustered around the display screens, well...

Imagine a disturbing cross between a hard-edged multifaceted and multi-spiked crystal and a flowing round-edged organic creature like a sea anemone. The two images shouldn't be able to occupy the same place in your mind's eye, but I can assure you that this is actually the closest description any of us who saw the impossible structure could come to putting its mind-twisting geometry into words. For one instant it would look like a crystal, then, without you even being aware of it having changed - if it had - it would appear to be soft-edged and flexible. None of us could bear to look at it for more than a few seconds without being forced to return our gaze to something - anything - solid and of this set of dimensions.

Its true size was impossible to fathom with nothing to compare it to in the display. One moment it would seem to be something you could hold in your hand - not that you'd want to - and the next you would swear it was the size of a space habitat. The computer showed a scale indicator that claimed to put it at some 300 yards at its widest aspect, but for all I could tell that could just as easily be a hardware glitch and its true size be fluctuating just as it appeared to.

The only thing about it that was not in dispute was its color. In the lightless depths of the ice-capped ocean, the clearly trans-dimensional apparition glowed with a ghostly pale green emanation that was flatly and rigidly monochromatic. It was a single, definite color, with no graduations caused by uneven lighting or any such effect. Clearly, the illumination was an inherent quality of its structure and not something imposed on it from outside.

The strangest thing about the whole structure, though, was the way it made the mind think there was more to it than the eye encompassed. It was an eerie, unsettling phenomenon caused by its extra dimensions, I'm sure. But knowing the origin of it didn't help any. Your eye still wanted to extend its lines off in directions that just don't exist for us.

"I don't think anyone *built* that," one of the crewmen said. "I think it grew that way."

"It does look sort of like a crystal," Capt. Panoss agreed. "Maybe crossed with a deep sea creature on steroids. But whatever it is, what I'd like to know is how it got here. It was before you joined us, Dale, but we were commissioned to do a mapping run of the sea floor down here not two years back, and there's no way we would have missed that. It had to have..."

Suddenly a violent lurch shook the entire sub, knocking all of us off our feet. Before we could do more than grab on to whatever handholds were available, the nose of the craft shot down sharply. My augmented strength and reflexes enabled me to avoid the fate of everyone else on the bridge, which was to be thrown into a tangle-limbed heap in the bottom of the pit was that was the up-ended control room.

The sub was nose down at about a 70-degree angle, I'd say, which was far more than it had ever been designed for. Alarms started sounding and flashing, but no one was in any position to do anything about what was causing them. I was learning - the hard way - the life aboard a submarine was vastly different from being in space, despite the overt similarities.

For one thing, there were no localized-gravity generating minz coils built into the superstructure, so all of us aboard were enslaved to the planetary gravity field. Down was always toward the planet's center of mass, no matter which direction or at what orientation the floor might be.

And, unlike my own ship and a fair number of Imperial Naval vessels, my implanted computer could not take control of this ship's systems.

The combination of these two facts kept me from being able to do anything, other than watch with a growing sense of horror, what was happening to us.

Even as I sought better hand and footholds

to anchor myself against the continuing tremors that persisted in trying to shake me loose and add me to the bruised pile of humanity down below, I managed to keep part of my attention on the display screens that still tracked and showed the mysterious undersea formation that, by all rights, should not exist anywhere in our dimensions.

And how could I not, when it was clear we were being drawn directly toward it. This was no illusion, making me think it was growing larger in the screens. Even without being able to see or access the sub's navigation or other systems, I could see the distance-to-target indicator on the visual display rapidly dwindling down to a very uncomfortable number.

We were on a collision course and there was nothing I could do about it. Even if I'd been firmly strapped into the pilot's seat, or whatever it's equivalent was on a submarine, I wouldn't have the faintest idea how to go about configuring its various systems to save us. I'd heard talk of dive planes and ballast tanks, but how to employ them was beyond me.

Fortunately for us all, someone else was there who was much more capable than I.

(We're being pulled down! Can you do anything?)

Of all the possible responses I could have gotten, none would have surprised me more than Sam's simple, ((I'm sorry, Sire, but I cannot.))

I was very nearly in shock. Here I was, just

moments away from a deadly crash in a crushing environment much more lethal than open space, and the immortal protector of the Imperial bloodline is telling me there's nothing he can do to save me.

Now, I'm not one to shy away from the thought of death. I've faced the possibility of my demise on any number of occasions. Yes, I've always had Sam there to run interference and block the Big Black, but I'm a realist. I know there are no guarantees. As powerful as Sam is, there are some situations where he is just as helpless as I am. For all his tremendous abilities, he has his own limitations, and I guess I always knew that one day I'd manage to get myself into a situation more dire than any of my ancestors in the Empire's thousand-year plus history. If any Tarkle was going to be the one who went too far for Sam to save, I just knew it would be me.

But I wasn't dead yet, and I had no intention of surrendering to that without exhausting every resource at my disposal. And part of my survival tool kit - the most important part, at that - is my intellect. In this one area, I might perhaps even surpass Sam.

(Why can't you do anything?) I asked. We were going down fast, but I estimated we had about two minutes until we collided with the big crystal, or whatever it really was.

((I cannot halt our descent or affect our course at all from within this gravity well.))

Okay, that much made sense. Sam is a creature of gravity. It was trivial for him to pull a starship around in space; all he had to do was get near it and allow some of his inherent gravity to trickle into this dimension. But if he were to do that underwater, on a planetary body, he would cause massive upheaval and potentially disastrous destruction. Once I thought about it, I realized that unleashing even a tiny fraction of a black hole's force within a planet's gravity well could not end well for that planet.

But wait a moment. Never before has Sam hesitated to take whatever measures were necessary to ensure my survival. Part of his nature is his existence not at a single point in time but across a range of times. If he was not doing anything, it was because he knew absolutely that I would survive regardless.

(So there's no danger?)

((I did not say that. You will, however, survive without any action on my part.))

(Oh, great.) I should have known better than to think I was going to get off scot-free. Sam will do anything at all to keep me alive - he's proven that on many occasions. What he is not so quick to do, however, is draw attention to himself for any reason short of that. He is absolutely fanatic about keeping his existence a secret, so he would rather me take all sorts of lumps then give himself away.

Capt. Panoss and the other crewmen were still trying to climb out of the bow and reach any of the sub's controls when we struck the crystal.

As for myself, I was seriously regretting not keeping my space armor on. Whatever was about to happen, I was sure I'd be better off in my shell than out of it.

CHAPTER 8

The first thing I noticed about the crash was that it didn't happen. And if you think it sounds confusing when I put it that way, just try to imagine how I felt experiencing it. There we were, in an uncontrolled plunge being pulled inexorably toward what appeared to be a solid structure many times the size of our vessel. The only monitors I could see showed us closing with increasing speed, and then the entire sub lost all power the instant of the unexpected impact.

I don't mean that main power went down and emergency systems kicked in. *All* powered equipment suddenly stopped working, including the gear that was supposed to take over in such a situation. And not just the sub's components, either. Even my electric implants went down. In the perfect darkness, my first confused thought was that I had indeed died, despite Sam's best efforts.

It was the voices of my companions, the sub's crew, that convinced me otherwise. They, too, were confused, but it seems to me they were better able to adjust to the new conditions than I was. My thinking was slow and fuzzy, like a significant part of my brain had just quit working. I heard the captain speaking, but I could only understand a few of his words. I was still wondering why everyone had suddenly started speaking an almost incomprehensible dialect when a couple of the crew activated chemical lights and it struck me that we were still alive and not in immediate danger.

It was then that I became even more confused as I realized that the weightlessness we were experiencing could not be accounted for by the total power failure. To me, who spends so much of my time in space, it was natural to associate the two. Only belatedly did I catch on to the fact that we had been under a natural gravity field.

The complete loss of all electrical power in every device, plus the loss of planetary gravity, could only add up to something being Very Wrong. But without my implants to assist my cognitive functions, I was at a loss to think of what to do first. I was so used to having a clearly defined list of appropriate responses to any situation instantly presented to my mind that without my neural implant I was almost paralyzed with confusion.

Well, even without my mental assistant I knew that I could always count on Sam. His very alien mind might not always come up with the same response as my human-programmed computer would, but at least he could never be disabled or taken from me.

Or so I thought.

Capt. Panoss and his crew didn't have to restrain me or anything like that, but I'll admit it was touch-and-go for the first few minutes after I discovered that I could get no response from Sam.

I first tried talking to him psionically. Now, I've been doing this longer than I've had any neural implants, so I know deep down that my silent communication with him is not dependent on any technology. Nonetheless, when I got no answer that way my next confused impulse was to call out aloud to him. Well, that got a response all right, but not the one I was hoping for.

The captain, whom was busy helping his crew deal with the unexpected weightlessness, happened to be closer to me than the others. When he heard my fairly quiet but frantic calls for a response, he naturally enough thought I was trying to use an implant to contact someone.

Without my translator working I could barely understand him, but from his tone and gestures I gathered that he was saying something along the lines of, "Mine isn't working either."

At least, that's what I make of it in hindsight. At the time, I was too busy freaking out over the lack of response from Sam to think very clearly about anything else. I mean, this is something I never, ever expected to happen, and so I was totally and completely unprepared to deal with it. I'm normally a sane and stable man, but everyone has his limits and mine had just been crossed.

I shouted out his name. I looked all around, going so far as to snatch a light stick out of a crewman's hand to help me see under consoles and in corners. I roughly shoved another man out of my way, with no regard for any injury I might cause, when he came between me and the hatch leading off the bridge.

The regular crew might have been too intimidated by my position or reputation to do anything, but to his credit the captain recognized the symptoms of stress-induced panic. He grabbed me in a bear hug from behind, pinning my arms to my sides. His feet must have been braced somehow, because he was able to control my movement without us both drifting away.

"Calm down, man!" he told me in clear, sharply pronounced words. "You have to chill out!"

Suddenly it struck me. I, Prince Edj, was giving in to panic. I, who has had it drilled into me all my life how to avoid thoughtless emotional reaction, was in the grip of just such a dangerous enemy. I should know better. The only excuse I can offer, inadequate as it is, is that nothing in my extensive training had ever suggested the scenario I found myself in.

I went slack in the captain's arms. "I'm with it now. Thanks."

And I was, too. Once my logical, rational mind took over for the unthinking animal, I began to assess our situation in light of all my training and experiences. Item: Sam was not responding. Okay, what could account for that? He would never voluntarily leave me, so either he had been destroyed or we had become separated. Since I just couldn't give any credence to him having been destroyed while any part of the universe continued to exist, and I was pretty sure the sub and all those of us in it did in fact still exist, I had to think something had happened to separate us.

Item: I lost touch with him at roughly the same time as we made contact with the extradimensional artifact. Now, I understand that Sam exists in several more dimensions than what we of our universe think of as normal space. But are these the only extra dimensions that there are? The scientists who claim to have a handle on these matters say no. Does that mean there are sets of dimensions where I can exist but he cannot? I have no idea. But I can't rule it out.

So if we had somehow been transported into the artifact's home space, it might follow that Sam would be unable to follow me.

Item: there was no gravity affecting us. This could mean we were in open space, far from any high-mass points, or we could be in free fall. Or, it suddenly struck me, we could be in a continuum where there was no such thing as gravity.

According to those same physicists who supposedly know such things, gravity is just one force among many, all of which have their origin in the mixture of dimensions unique to each local universe. In the greater multiverse, there are some realms where the physical constants are not the same values as we have measured. That much has been proven experimentally. It's why we can sidestep the limit imposed by the speed of light by traveling hyperspace. So if we had somehow entered one where there was no such thing as the force of gravity, it would mean that a black hole would be unable to exist.

So was there any way of determining if we were in such a strange place? Well, gravity is responsible for more than just the creation of black holes. Without it, no stars or galaxies would form, either. Would a simple look outside disprove all my gossamer-threaded reasoning and plunge me right back into the depths of mindless terror? There was only one way to find out, and I've never been one to put off doing something just because it might be unpleasant or force me to rethink something.

One thing I had noticed as I floated there lost in my thoughts was that the speech of the crewmen, at first all but incomprehensible to me without the aid of my neuroware's translator function, was beginning to sound closer to something I could understand. Maybe my brain had a better faculty for languages and accents than I had been giving myself credit for and it just needed a few minutes on its own to prove it to me. In any case, I was glad to be able to understand most of what was being said around me again, even if I wasn't thrilled about what was being said.

No one had any more clue as to what had happened to us than I did. Not surprising, I suppose. At least the sub itself was still intact. Capt. Panoss had sent men out to check our status, and no damage was being reported. It seemed clear to everyone by this time that whatever had occurred, we had not crashed into the big, glowing whatever-it-was.

We had several more questions that were not so easily answered, though. Setting aside the whole issue of how we would return to where we left, the foremost issue was the mystery of what had happened to our power. Aboard any ship, whether immersed in sea or space, the single most important system is the electricity supply. Without that, every other issue pales beside the necessity of restoring the means of powering the myriad subsystems by which a ship keeps its occupants alive and enables them to navigate and move, among other things.

I had a feeling I could at least explain what had happened, even if we would still be at a loss as to what to do about it, if I could just make one simple observation. "I have a theory," I told the men on the bridge, "that can account for a lot, but I need to get a look outside to confirm it. Are there any portholes I can peep through?"

"An explainin' would do mighty for calmin' nerves, sure enough," the 1st mate replied. "But as for what you're wantin', well, it ain't not possible, but it won't be free-float either. None at all."

The quizzical look on my face must have told him as much as my silence did about how much I understood that reply, for he chuckled and said more clearly, "Sorry I am. Meaning that there is an eye-hole, but gettin' to its where with no power'll be a vexing task for sure."

"What he's talkin'," Capt. Panoss explained, his speech only slightly more understandable to me, "is there ain't but one porthole in the whole sub, on account of that bein' a mighty weak spot in the pressure hull. So it's in the lower airlock, a part of the emergency docking and retrieval system. And that's sealed off behind to pressure hatches. It's the opening of them that'll be the problem, without power."

One of the other crewmen, after looking to the captain for permission, then said, "I don't think it's even doable to open 'em, what with them being electrical driven and locked down."

Panoss shook his head. "Normally it wouldn't, but I'm thinking that if a man was to unbolt the right access panel an' dig deep enough he could free the locking levers. Then we could break out the manual pump for the hydraulic cutter-pryers from the rescue kit and force the doors open thatta way."

The crewman nodded his head. "Yeah, I can see that workin'. You want I should get started, sir?"

I think that final 'sir' was only added as an

afterthought, because of my presence. The crew just did not strike me as being very military-minded. Nonetheless, when it came time to man the hydraulic pump there was no shortage of volunteers. Perhaps it had more to do with it being the only activity going on in what was an admittedly very scary situation, but everyone crowded around the slowly-opening door and yet not one of them gave voice to the fear that had to be close to the surface of every mind there.

Finally, the second set of doors parted and the captain and I gained entry into the lower airlock's final chamber. There, as promised, awaited the sub's only window to the outside world. No less than any other man aboard, I had built up quite an appreciable level of anticipation while waiting for this moment. I would at least finally have more data on which to base my theories, and in such a desperate situation as we were in, our total lack of information was the worst state imaginable. Knowing *anything* would be better than knowing nothing.

The porthole loomed just ahead, and I had barely gotten my first glimpse of green-glowing artifact against a stygian, starless void when the entire sub again began to tremble and shake even worse than before. If I hadn't already been holding on to a brace, I could have ended up in as bad of a state as the captain, which was just about as bad as could be.

There was once a time - now over three decades past - when I naively believed that no one ever really suffered life-threatening injuries. Raised as I was with only the highest-quality and best-maintained *everything* surrounding me, accidents just did not occur. And anything that did happen to anyone I ever heard of caused only minor, easily repairable damage, if even that. Between the safety of our tried-and-true technology and the medical miracles worked by physicians, there was just no such thing in my young mind as a truly dangerous accident.

My eyes were opened to the falseness of my perception of this aspect of reality while I was on an extended training session on an exceptionally rugged and unforgiving young rocky world. My classmates and I were being taught to climb steep mountains using only manual equipment, such as ropes and pitons. No anti-gravity lifts or powered winches for us boys, oh no. It was all muscle and sweat, and it was very tiring on our young bodies. So tiring, in fact, that it caused one of my companions to neglect to test one of the anchors he inserted into a crack in the rock face. When the next boy came up and attached his safety line to that, he assumed that it would hold his weight if he slipped. Well, he did and it didn't. I'll never forget the sight of his head splitting open like an overripe melon when he hit the scree below. Even if there had been a medic right beside where he landed, he couldn't have been saved. Once a human head sustains that kind of catastrophic damage, nothing in the multiverse can help.

Capt. Thos Panoss was another such unfortunate victim of circumstances. The crewman who left the massive steel hydraulic cutters floating beside the second hatch cannot entirely blame himself for what happened when the totally unexpected happened and the sub began flinging everything inside it around like so many pebbles in a primitive shaman's gourd rattle.

And even then, randomness played the deciding role in the tragedy, for if either the captain's head or the heavy tool hadn't ended up precisely where they had when gravity returned and brought the two together, things probably wouldn't have been nearly so bad.

Now, some people might say that for a man to be killed by such an incredible string of occurrences must mean he had ticked off a god or be due his fate from some cosmic law of retribution. If there are any such principals or principles operating in reality, I am blissfully unaware of them. All I can say is that the good Captain had the worst random luck of his life that day, and it just happened to be on the last day of his life.

The return of gravity wasn't an isolated occurrence, either, as was made clear by the reactivation of all our electrical equipment, including my implants that had been shut down. Only for a split second did I wonder if we were still in that other, odd dimension and merely somehow had our accustomed conveniences restored to us, for Sam's oh-so-welcome mental voice told me we were indeed back where we belonged.

((I am here, Sire. I regret that I could not accompany you, but I knew you would return safely at this time.))

Coming from anyone else that statement would have sounded like nothing more than wishful thinking, but since Sam doesn't need to dope himself up with Peek to see certain aspects of the future, I simply accepted that as the truth that was.

(Glad to hear it. How long were we gone?)

Now, you may think it odd that I even had to ask such a question but consider this: I had just been to the home continuum of a trans-dimensional entity that was obviously somehow displaced from my own dimension's time stream. And since the scientists tell us that time is a relative thing, I am open to the possibility that its rate of passage can vary not only according to how fast one is moving but also according to where in the multiverse one is. So it makes perfect sense to think that just because I seemed to experience a couple of hours 'over there', the same length of time need not have passed for someone left behind.

((From my perspective you were gone roughly four hours. And may I say that it is very astute of you to realize that there was a time differential involved.))

Oh wow. He must really have been worried about me. Sam almost *never* compliments me for anything. That he did so then told me just how much my absence bothered him. I wish things hadn't been so hectic just then, because I really wish I'd had time to tease him about it, but as things were I merely accepted it and moved on.

"Is anyone injured?" I asked and was greatly relieved to find out that the second-most serious injury our abrupt transition back to our continuum had caused was a sprained ankle to one of the crewmen.

"Good. Then I suggest -" A quick glance at Kiata confirmed that he had no objection to my taking control of his ship and men, "- that we get main power back up and put some distance between us and... whatever the void that thing was."

No one had any problem with that idea. I don't think any of us wanted a repeat trip out of our dimension, and the best way to prevent that from happening seemed to be to get us as far away from our current location in as expeditious a manner as possible.

The sub's crew all knew their jobs. It was only a matter of a few minutes before I felt the deck under my feet take on a distinct upward tilt, which relieved me to an inordinate degree. I was still more than a little shaken up at having lost contact with Sam and thus facing the very real possibility of my demise.

Nothing was said about the fact that I was responsible for the death of Capt. Panoss. No amount of arguing that accidents happen can change the fact that it was because of me that he was where he was when he was. The cold, hard truth is that he would still be alive if I hadn't called for him and his ship. I knew that and was willing to take full responsibility for it, even if his crewmates would not say anything.

Among a purely military crew I would have put such a lack of reaction down to good discipline and training. Here, though, I suspect it had everything to do with who I am, and that's just not right. If Jed Ecnirp had caused a death, everyone would have jumped all over him. But not Prince Edj, oh no. Everyone is way too wrapped up in how they think they should act around royalty to even consider that we are people, too, with the same emotional needs as themselves.

With a start, I suddenly realized that I had been standing there lost in my thoughts for the last few minutes. Admittedly, there wasn't anything that I needed to be doing right then, but still, I had no business is zoning off like a Tabloran zonck out filter-feeding. Especially not when we were still in a potentially very dangerous situation.

There seems to be nothing that could be done with the captain's body other than cover it with the foil blanket I found in an emergency supplies locker, so once that was accomplished I returned to the bridge. First Mate Kiata looked relieved when I did, and I pegged him as one who was much more comfortable not being in charge. Some officers are like that, and I'll admit that the Empire needs both types; in all things balance and all of that.

And me, I'm used to being in control. It goes with the whole Prince thing. "Ship's status?"

"We are mobile and life-support is fully functional." Kiata paused, and I knew then what the reason for the look of distress that had momentarily crossed his face when I first entered the bridge was.

"But... " I prompted, having a pretty good idea of what was coming.

"But we are operating on reserve power only. The main reactor is not restarting, and we don't know why."

I hate being right. I'd just *known* he was going to say that, and sure enough, he had. Now, I'm a spaceman. On a starship, the loss of your main power source is a Very Big Deal. So many systems require a lot more juice than backups can provide that you really don't ever want to hear that your reactor won't start.

Some of that ingrained reaction must have shown through on my expression, for the first mate hurriedly said, "It's not that big a deal, Sire. Unlike a spacecraft, we have low-power alternatives. We can operate for weeks on our reserves. The only real need for the reactor is to power our reactionless drive and reactive shields. We are still capable of moving using conventional water jets."

I allowed them to witness my sigh of relief. "That's good. That's very good, but I'll admit that I'd feel better with full power available. You have no idea why the reactor stalled?"

At a glance from his superior, the crewman running the ship's engineering console spoke up. "Well, Sire, according to the diagnostics I ran there is nothing at all wrong with it. I can only suppose that whatever it is we just went through did something to some vital part of it." He shook his head. "I'm sorry, Sire. C... Captain Panoss was our fusion engineer."

That earned a moment of silence, after which I said, "So, reserve power it is. I want to collect as much information as possible about that... thing... as we leave it behind. Run every sensor you've got, but put us on a course back to the surface and open water beyond the ice cap. I'll not put any of you at further risk."

I could see that a couple of them wanted to say something about it being their honor to serve me or some such thing, so I shook my head. "No, even one life lost is unacceptable. Captain Panoss will be given an imperial funeral with full honors, but I cannot express how much I regret the necessity for it. The rest of you have all earned medals from the hand of the Emperor himself for your help to me and willingness to risk your lives." I paused there, aware that every remaining man on the submarine was crowded into the bridge by this point. After looking each of them in the eye, I said, "I thank you all, but whatever I do next, I'll do alone."

Now, I'm just plain not used to being contradicted. I mean, it's just not usually done even when those around me know me only as Jed the freighter pilot. For someone to dispute what Prince Edj says is a situation that has only happened a very few times, and never since I reached adulthood.

Yet it happened then and there, and while I can't fault the man who uttered it, I do wish the situation that gave him cause to hadn't come up.

"Uh, Sire, I'm afraid that's not going to be so easy."

That certainly got everyone's attention. In a heartbeat, every eye was focused on the man at the sub's scanner station. Mack Turner, I remember he was called. Despite the large gold hoop earring in his left ear and bald head, he'd never struck me as being overly self-confident. I do believe these were the first words he said to me the whole time I've been aboard.

We all knew he must have had a good reason, and unfortunately, we were right.

"Sensors show a spider-kraken has locked onto us, Sire. ETA about 5 minutes."

Oh, crap. Somewhere in the back of my mind, I'd known that there was a danger in using the ship's backup propulsion, but with everything else on my mind I only offer the fact that a spaceman does not normally think in terms of how much noise his vessel makes as a mitigating factor. I should have, I know, I've been told, and it was my responsibility. But what can I say? As certain members of the Imperial Court are always quick to point out, I'm not exactly perfect.

Whether I would have tried to find an alternative to the loud water-jets had I remembered the threat of the sea monsters was irrelevant by this time. I hadn't, so we had to deal with it.

"Any chance it will ignore us now that we are quiet?"

Kiata shook his head. "These things are relentless hunters. Once something's attracted their attention, they are locked onto it like... well, like you are on finding that thief, D'Orneo, Sire."

Not good, not good at all. "Okay, this sub's built to deal with them. What are our options?"

"Without full power, the water jets are our only means of propulsion, and even the active noise cancellation can't cope with that. And the more noise we make, the madder it drives the beast. It'll snare us and drag us deeper. Fortunately, the bottom around here is nowhere near our crush depth."

Good, good. "Okay, then what?"

He sighed softly. "Then we sit, anchored to the biggest rocks the thing can find, until we either cut ourselves loose or, or..." He looked down at the deck and shook his head. "We are the only sub on the planet really capable of dealing with them," he added, almost whispering.

In his defense, I'd like to think that Mr. Kiata is usually a competent-enough leader, him being the first mate and all. And he had, after all, just witnessed the pointless death of his captain, so I'll choose to attribute his loss of poise to that and not to any inherent flaw in the man's character.

A quick glance around the bridge reinforced the idea, for the faces I saw mirrored his defeated look. It was clearly time for another patented Prince Edj save.

"No," I stated clearly and firmly. When I speak in that tone, even galactic-scale forces of nature have been known to sit up and take notice, so I knew these men had no choice but to take heart by my sure pronouncement. "I don't have time to wait for rescue, and I sure don't intend to do nothing."

Although what I *could* do, I didn't know yet. (Alright, you force of nature. Options?)

((From in here, not many. I could attempt to disrupt the creature's nervous system, but any sufficiently powerful emanations from me would undoubtedly wreak havoc on your vessel's electronics. This would not harm you if you were first to don your armor, but it would likely reveal my presence. Since your life is not presently in danger, I would suggest exploring other options.))

Wow, Sam must still be reeling from his loss of me during my little extra-dimensional jaunt for him to be talking like that. I mean, he usually just flatly refuses to do anything that might give himself away. And if he was going to keep being so downright accommodating, who was I to pass up such an unusual opportunity?

(Okay, so what if I were to get you outside?)

((I would make a very unpleasant pill for the beast to swallow.))

My armor carries several small remote viewing drones. The standard version of this handy little globe only contains a small self-destruct charge, which has been employed by many soldiers to take out a single enemy or a tactically-important piece of electronics. There is no way, though, that one could produce anywhere near a large enough blast to kill such a huge beast as a spider-kraken.

I know this, and most Imperial Marines notice. The remaining crew of the *Mercy Mia*, however, were easy to convince that a single drone, ejected through the airlock, could and did. Note to self: be sure to have a supply of self-propelled high explosive munitions delivered to the crew. They'll find them very handy the next time they go kraken hunting.

CHAPTER 9

"So where did it come from?" Governor Svensson asked. We were once again meeting in his over-opulent office, my first stop after a quick pit stop aboard the Wah.

"Well, figuring that out is likely to fuel more than a few doctoral dissertations. You know what academics are like."

"As a matter of fact, I do," Olaf grinned. "Oh, I certainly do. They can go on and on, dragging out the tiniest detail. Why, I remember once when I asked for a study on the effects of chewing gum on betting habits... But I digress. Please forgive me, Your Highness."

I offered the planet's highest elected official a small smile of kinship. We could both spend the rest of the day exchanging examples of how single-minded scholars can be. "But fortunately for us, it seems that we don't need to know precisely what higher dimension it came from to be able to send it back there. At least, that's what the eggheads back on Alphum think."

"That's great… I think. If you'll forgive my pre-sumptuousness, Sire, I built my career around my ability to read people and I suspect from what I'm seeing in you right now that I'm not going to be very happy with whatever it is you haven't told me yet."

((Oh, he's good, all right. There are several bureaus back in the capital he'd be a natural head for.))

I chuckled inwardly. Sam doesn't often comment on political matters, but whenever he does, he invariably calls it dead on. Perhaps Svensson's talents would indeed make him a valuable asset in the higher echelons of the Imperial government, but a valid argument could also be made that he was sorely needed right where he was, keeping a jaundiced eye on a planet full of professional gamblers and con men.

"I'm afraid you may be right. You see, they think the… whatever it is has managed to some-how get itself stuck here in our continuum. Sort of like the Blarian donknaff that's always clawing a hole just big enough for its head through the shell of giant smarr eggs and then getting stuck when it eats so much that its jowls balloon out."

"So we need to grease the whole, is that what you're saying?"

"Uh-huh. But in this case, the KY Jelly is going to have to be squirted on by an array of hyper-space motivators."

"I hate it when I'm right. This is sounding less

and less nice."

I couldn't help but give him a wry grin. "But wait, there's more. According to the data of the rescue sub's systems collected, the thing is rather firmly attached to your planet's center of mass. In other words, it's not liable to go anywhere in this dimension that the planet itself doesn't."

If it was possible for Olaf to look even more crestfallen, he managed it as the realization of what I was saying sank in.

"But... if you can't drag it up into space first... you can't be seriously thinking about opening a hole into hyperspace *under my ocean*. I... I... Look, Your Highness, I'm about to farthest thing there is in the 99 Stars from a hyperspace engineer, but even I know that there are all kinds of Really Bad Things that are supposed to happen when you do that too close to a planet. And I'm pretty sure that the ocean floor under an ice cap qualifies as too close."

((It's good to see that at least one of you thinks this is a bad idea.))

(Oh, hush. You're just miffed because this whole extra-dimensional thing doesn't rely on you for a change. Is my little black hole buddy feeling left out?"

Wow. I finally did it. For once, Sam had no smart come-back. Maybe he does have something like feelings after all.

"And that's why it's going to be so expensive to take care of," I told the governor. If Sam wanted to pretend to be hurt, he could just get used to sulking alone.

"Oh, how did I know you were going there?"

"Oh, probably because you know as well as I do that a planet is responsible for itself in internal matters. And face it, since Peek is confined to this planet and this planet alone, dealing with it clearly falls under the 'local solutions to local problems' clause of your world's Imperial Charter." I took a sip of the excellent coffee to give him a chance to swallow that, then added, "But, that's not to say that Villalba won't be positively flooded with highly-paid hyperspace and force field experts from all over the Empire. And I would guess it will take them quite some time to work out how to properly shield the affected area, not to mention actually rigging the field generators and support equipment in such a unique environment. Plus, I'm thinking there will be all sorts of other researchers coming in to get their own look at things. Yep, it looks like there ought to be quite a bit of profit to be made, what with the need to house and entertain so many. I'd bet that whoever arranged the on-site accommodations could come out well ahead of the house, in fact."

Now, I have a pretty good sense of what drives a man, so I could tell that Governor Svensson was not all about personal profit. But still, no one at his level is totally averse to making an extra credit or three in the right circumstances.

He wasn't. While I didn't actually see credit signs light up in his eyes, the idea was certainly there.

"As it happens, I do own partial interest in a touring casino ship. If it should be found to be close to the southern ice cap, well, that would be just plain convenient. For the scientists and all, that is."

"Of course. So, now that that's all in the proper hands, there is still the matter that drew me to your world to start with."

"Yes, of course." He paused a moment, obviously accessing his implant. "The psi interrogator is due to arrive at 7:30 tomorrow morning, and all 33 of former governor D'Orneo's associates have been brought to a holding facility here on Triffin. Are there any other arrangements I can see to, Sire?"

I thought for a moment but couldn't come up with anything more he could do to help. When I shook my head, he said, "As I suspected. Well then, in that case, my dear wife has instructed me to extend an invitation for you to join us at our residence for a simple, private dinner tonight."

"Well, sir, 'simple' and 'private' are two of my favorite words. Tell your lady I gratefully accept."

Ella Svensson was indeed a lady. Tall and regal, she wore her simple maroon dress with grace and dignity. Yet even in the midst of all the wealth a mega-rich planet like Villalba could produce, she seemed singularly unaffected by its trappings. Her jewelry was limited to a single diamond wedding band and a set of ruby-pearl earrings, and her manner was warm and friendly. My status didn't faze her at all. Indeed, I firmly believe she would have been just as gracious a host to Jed the trader as she was to Prince Edj. A woman like that doesn't come along very often, and Olaf was a lucky man to have found her.

Dinner was, as promised, both simple and private. Mrs. Svensson made no secret that her staff had prepared it, but she herself served the freshly caught sea bass and accompanying sides. Our conversation, too, was refreshingly free of the usual politics and palace talk that I positively abhor. Both Svenssons, I learned, are quite knowledgeable enthusiasts of the game of multidimensional chess, and upon discovering that I also share a fondness for the ancient game, we spent most of the evening discussing strategy and dissecting the recent Imperial playoff series. I was somewhat astonished to learn, although it really should have come as no surprise to me, that Ella is able to hold her own in a 7-D match, while both the governor and I rarely play well above five dimensions. Of course, she only admitted to this after thoroughly trouncing each of us men in the inevitable after-dinner matches. As I said before, Olaf did well when he caught his wife.

That evening I slept in a guest room in the gubernatorial mansion, awakening earlier than I had expected the following morning with my head full of anticipation for the results of the upcoming interrogations. Finally I might learn where to find that rat D'Orneo and Melanada. I couldn't wait.

I had to wait, and wait, and wait.

First there was the delay while the interrogator had himself and all the prisoners moved to a ship - the floating-on-water kind - so that there would be less of what he called 'psychic pollution' to interfere with his readings.

And then, even after all this had been done, I still had to wait while a team of police put together a video montage of old D'Orneo footage showing him with as many of his convicted cronies as possible. This was done, at the interrogator's insistence, so that his subjects could be forced to watch it and thus be thinking about the former governor and their association with him. I was not happy at all when I learned about this delay, to say the least. Why, I demanded, had this not been put together during the week the psi was in transit?

The answer was, in short, bureaucratic ineptitude. It turned out that the psionic was not informed why his services were needed until he arrived on Villalba. When I rather pointedly pointed out that he should have known, what with him being a *psychic* after all, no one around me had any response other than a few groans.

Finally, though, the prisoners were deemed to

be physically far enough away from enough other minds that the mind-reader could work on them and the actual interrogations could begin. I almost blew a gasket when I found out just what form this would take. I'd thought it would be simply a matter of the psychic - Jorge Mendoza, I finally learned was his name - looming over each prisoner and mentally reaching into his head and pulling out whatever he knew about D'Orneo's secrets.

Boy was I wrong.

There was nothing quick and dirty about it. Each crony was given a drug that made him focus all his attention on whatever was before him, and set down to watch the D'Orneo video. Mendoza would stand behind him with hands on his head for somewhere between a quarter to half an hour, silently probing and listening in on the subject's thoughts. Then, between subjects, he would take breaks lasting sometimes that much longer. Clearing his mind, he said, and consolidating his results.

After two full days of watching this non-progress I was about ready to burst into the room with my quick-staff and go medieval on them when the Mendoza finally announced he had something tangible for me. It turned out that D'Orneo had, on many occasions, entertained none other than Jonah Merkel himself. He, if by chance you do not recognize the name, is the grandson of the real-life pirate Tibbon Merkel, the founder of Merkel's Drift and inspiration for that whole 'Pirates of the Void' movie series. And the Merkel Drift, as I'm sure you know, is that infamous and notorious den of interstellar thieves and outlaws that somehow always manages to avoid destruction by any of the galactic powers.

That might be about to change, though.

If Jonah Merkel had been welcome on Villalba, It could only mean that he and D'Orneo were tight. No real surprise, that, come to think of it. It is said that anything in the galaxy can be bought or sold on Merkel's Drift, if one is accepted by the criminal element, and there was no bigger criminal in the Empire than D'Orneo.

They *had* to still be in contact. If anyone could lead me to my prey, it would be Merkel.

Now all I had to do was find someone who could lead me to the Drift and gain me admittance.

Not even Imperial intelligence knew where the mobile habitat was currently located. It is known to roam the lawless void far outside the Empire, but finding it has never been a top priority among law-enforcement agencies. Since its information brokering function can be accessed by anyone in possession of the proper codes and clearances, the intelligence arms of all the local galactic governments have, up to now, been content to leave it alone. It does, after all, provide a needed service to the galaxy at large, for both criminals and undercover authorities.

But I can't provide Merkel the proper incentives for cooperation over the phone. Some things just have to be handled up close and personal. So getting there became on my next objective. I left Mendoza to finish up his interrogations while I made my arrangements. I'd have liked to have his particular abilities available when I confront Merkel, but the risk of bringing him along with me was too great, given how I was going to have to get there.

That's right - I had no choice but to call on my old friends Twilla and Marek. I was almost afraid to contemplate the price the Order of the Eternals would demand for their help this time, but it was either use the resources at hand or waste who knows how much more time cultivating another entry into Merkel's private little kingdom. And while the thought of simply throwing the full might of the Imperial Navy at him was tempting, it was much more likely to cost lots of lives for no gain than to net me the information only a one-on-one with Merkel himself would get me.

No, this was most certainly a situation that called for the utmost subtlety, at least as far as getting me that meeting with the man. Of course, once I got to him I could afford to be as unsubtle as I cared to, an outcome that I freely admit I found myself looking forward to with unmitigated longing. I do so enjoy cleansing the galaxy of unsavory characters.

"Well, well, what a positively unexpected surprise. I honestly did not expect to hear from you again, Your Highness." Twilla's voice over the comm was all sweetness and light, completely belying the monstrous reality of her being.

"And in truth, I never expected to need to call upon you again. However, your Emperor requires your services."

"Ooh, so formal! Did you hear that, Marek? Our Emperor requires our services. I do believe our friend the prince thinks he can persuade us to aid him in some fashion by calling upon some imagined sense of loyalty or obligation to his crown."

I suppose I could have argued along that line for a bit, but it wouldn't have done any good. I know how the Eternals feel about all governments and authorities outside themselves: namely, that they are as far above such common, mortal rules as a man is above the hierarchy of an ant colony. Their loyalty extends to the other members of their Order and not a micrometer farther. No, appealing to them on any such level was, at the very least, a waste of breath, and almost certainly would be turned by them into another blood debt by the time all was said and done.

Knowing this, I decided to cut straight to the meat of the matter, so to speak. "Don't worry. You'll still get your pound of flesh." I hated to give in to their inhumane inhuman demands, but at least doing so right up front allowed me to stay in control.

"Go on."

"Here's how it's going to be. You will accompany me to Merkel's Drift and help me gain access to Jonah Merkel. In return for this and all your help earlier I'll see to it that your Order is allowed to operate a line of casinos here on Villalba where *fully-informed, willing* clients may wager their own flesh against appropriate rewards."

That hooked them, as I'd known it would. A truism of rulership down through the ages has always been that since people are going to do things you don't want them to despite your best efforts to stop them, you can at least make them do it your way and under your control and pay taxes on it.

"Your proposal highly intrigues me," Twilla replied immediately. It was clear to me that she wanted to lock it in post-haste. "Yet I must point out that the journey there may not be as you are envisioning. There are strict rules in place regarding what ships are allowed to approach the Drift. Under no circumstances would your personal vessel be granted access. Should you somehow learn the current coordinates - which neither Marek nor I know, I assure you - your ship would be destroyed with no questions asked. Their policy on this is very strict."

Not good, not good at all, because one thing was certain - after the conclusion of my talk with Merkel I will most assuredly want to leave in nothing less than a fast hurry.

"All right, then," I said, bowing to the inevitable. "How would you suggest we proceed?"

"Since I presume you will want to have your ship nearby, we should take it from here and rendezvous with one of ours that is cleared to approach. We'll leave your vessel a short hyper-jump away. I have to ask now - are you intending to portray yourself as the prince, the trader, or the Eternal?"

Without allowing my expression to change, I grinned inside. Say what you will about them, Revenants will always angle to increase your debt to them. And in an opponent, predictable is good, for it can often be used against them.

"A little bit of each, actually. Neither the prince nor the trader would be allowed aboard the Drift, so your Order will once again claim me as your own initially. And no, you will not receive any additional payment or concessions for this. The deal for the casinos covers *all* debts you may imagine me to incur during this mission, as well as all of my previous debts. Period."

She shook her two-faced head. "Not acceptable. Whether Merkel himself survives his encounter with you or not, it will be obvious that we helped you gain access to him. This will negatively affect the Order's trade with the remaining Drifters. I myself cannot commit the entire Order to such a destructive course of action."

A lopsided but not entirely unattractive smile stole across her faces. "But I will certainly pass your request on to our Coordinating Council. I'm sure the Eldest will be very interested in your offer."

That much, at least, I'd fully expected, for she was entirely correct. Why I - or, more precisely, Sam - could indeed destroy the entire place, my visit probably won't end with that happening. And that being the case, whoever is left there will know that any disruption I caused was enabled by the Revenants bringing me there. Ergo, not a good thing as far as their trade is concerned. And while a good argument could be made for why I would *want* to disrupt so much trade in illegal, untaxed goods, the simple fact of the matter is that such business will always be conducted by members of a certain class of society. It is better that it be done where the authorities at least know something about it, rather than completely off the radar, as it were.

And all that being the case, I had a ready answer waiting for just such an objection.

"That's fine - take it to your Council. And be sure to mention the fact that your Order's ability to continue to operate within the Empire of the 99 Stars hinges on your undertaking this mission." My voice went as cold as the interstellar medium as I told her, "You do not want to try me on this. I will allow nothing to stand between me and my goal here. *Nothing.*"

Less than two hours later I had a reply. Six hours after that, Twilla, Marek and I were docking the *Wah* in the interior hold of one of the Order's large cargo vessels.

When I play hardball, I play to win.

CHAPTER 10

The captain of *Far Horizons 17* introduced himself to me by the simple name 'Nemo', which he explained meant 'nobody'. I thought he could more accurately have called himself 'everybody', since it seemed like he had parts from about that many people, but I kept that opinion to myself. He was tall and broad, which I suppose was so he could fit more pieces in. His manner was aloof and coldly superior.

"You have been granted passage aboard my vessel, but know that neither your lineage, nor the Eldest's patronage, set you apart in my eyes from any other donor. No special honors will be accorded you and any debts you incur will be paid in full. Do I make myself clear?"

Now, I'm not really one to insist on folks treating me special just because of who I am, but at the same time, there are limits on how much merde I'll put up with.

"I'll grant that this is your ship, Captain, but

beyond basic customs pertaining to that, I want you to be very clear about something. I am Prince Edj Tarkle, and no one demands anything of me. You will accord me the respect that is my due in that regard, and also as one whose physical prowess and martial capabilities are as far beyond yours as you are above the common citizens upon whom you prey. Have I made myself perfectly clear?"

Yep, I certainly chose the right tactic to use in dealing with this smug bastard. Revenants are all, each and every one, obsessed with maintaining the illusion of their invulnerability and superiority over everyone else in the universe. And the higher an individual rises within their Order's internal hierarchy, the more this means to him, for rank is most often gained, held or lost by dint of physical combat.

I could tell that my only chance of securing anything resembling a peaceful trip for myself was to immediately set the record straight about who was the baddest of the bad aboard.

The docking bay that held the *Wah* could easily have fit two other ships her size in as well. Besides myself and 'my' two Revenants, there were five others. Nemo hadn't introduced his officers, but I could tell despite their lack of anything resembling uniforms that that's what they were. It didn't concern me that I might have to fight all of them, but if it came down to that I'd rather have plenty of room to maneuver. The big, open bay would serve just fine.

Capt. Nemo wasn't carrying any obvious weapons, but I didn't think for a nanosecond that he was unarmed or defenseless. Revenants *never* were, and especially not a ship captain unwillingly taking on such a unique passenger.

My quick-staff extended even as my hands slid down its length. In well under a second it went from being an innocent-seeming cylinder hanging from my belt to a 6-ft long instrument of fury with its business end intent on shattering Nemo's upper right arm.

That didn't happen.

Oh, my form was perfect and my aim true. The weighted end of my weapon struck his humerus dead on. The problem was what happened after that. A rapidly moving object impacting a motionless target should transfer an amount of energy equal to its mass times its speed, and the smaller the area of contact is the greater the damage usually is. The impact should have shattered his arm, since Nemo just stood there and let me take a swing at him with no attempt to counter or evade my blows.

But no matter how quickly or how hard I swung, the strikes lost all their momentum the instant they made contact. No kinetic energy was transferred to him at all as far as I could tell. There was not so much as a slight warming of the impact sites visible in the IR spectrum. If he'd been encased in a motion-damping force field I would have seen at least a transient heating effect. Once again the fabled Revenant invulnerability defied detection or explanation.

After allowing me to see that my attacks could not harm him, Nemo made his first move. Displaying reflexes and muscle speed that would put a hyped-up, 'borged-out' black belt to shame, he suddenly reached out and grabbed my staff as I executed a side swing while taking a step toward him. Normally, even if an opponent was fast enough to actually pull this off, all this would have accomplished was getting him a handful or two of broken bones.

Not Nemo. He grabbed and pivoted on his left leg, trying to gain possession of my weapon and fling me away simultaneously.

It didn't work.

My grip is the result of some of the best cyber-augment work available anywhere in the galaxy. No one disarms me unless I allow it.

So while maintaining my hold on the weapon, I took another step and then brought both feet up and around in a kick that could have felled a Sovoran gorilla.

And, just like everything else that came into physical contact with the nova-blasted Revenant, instantly lost all my momentum when it connected.

Now, I'm used to hitting soft targets, and I'm used to hitting hard targets. With my enhanced reflexes I've never had trouble adjusting on the fly when my target turned out to be the opposite of what I expected. And part of this, I know now, is because every target I've ever hit has reacted in a well-known, predictable manner.

When my feet neither rebounded nor continued moving with the target, I lost precious nanoseconds basically going, "What the freak?"

I mean, for that split-second none of my rather extensive training or imperial gray combat software knew what to do when I just came to a dead stop in mid-air.

Nemo had no such problem. In a flash, before I'd even started to react, he let go of the weapon to shove upward and out with both hands. And his impact lost none of its tremendous energy. I must have been thrown backward twenty feet if it was an inch.

At least the physics of my flight we're back in the realm of the predictable, so I had time to position myself to make it proper landing.

And I would have, too, if the wall of the bay hadn't been about 18 feet from where I'd started.

(That was *not* how I thought that would go,) I told Sam in quicktime as I sprang to my feet. (Do you have any clue as to how he's doing that inertia-canceling trick?)

((I do not. I detect no energy sources in or on his body, nor are there any external field projectors shielding him.))

I took a two-handed pole vaulter's grip near one end of my staff and charged Nemo.

(Well, I still have to teach him not to mess with Imperial royalty. Be ready to flashbang.)

Normal pole vaulting requires two things if it is to be done effectively. One is, of course, a pole of some length. That I had. In fact, even as I rushed my opponent, my staff extended to its maximum length of some 10 feet. The other mandatory component is a secure point on the ground on which to plant the end of said pole to arrest its forward motion and act as a pivot point. Without such, there can be no real pole-vaulting action.

The hangar deck was conspicuously deficient in any such convenient stops. This fact would have deterred any normal aspiring pole-vaulter, but yours truly is anything but boringly normal, thank you very much. And, more importantly in this situation, so were my equipment and available resources.

It was the unexpectedness of these upon which I was counting.

Absent anything on the deck upon which to pivot, my charge could only be interpreted by Nemo as some sort of blunt-tipped spear rush. So in response, he positioned himself with his feet wide and arms spread so as to be able to dodge to either side and probably grab the staff again.

Such a posture would have put him in good stead had I actually been doing what he expected. Against what I was really doing, though, that was about the worst way he could have been standing.

As I approached what both my instincts and

the programming in my neural implant agreed was the optimal point, I did two things. I mentally told Sam 'now' while simultaneously activating the surprise in the leading end of my staff. With its pseudo-mass drastically increased, the tip was suddenly much more attracted to the gravity generator somewhere below the deck.

It thunked down quite solidly and my mass and momentum did the rest. While Nemo was flash blinded and disoriented from Sam's super firecracker imitation going off right in front of his face, I flew in a parabolic arc that landed me squarely on his shoulders.

And *this* time I was ready for what would happen when I hit him.

With no inertia acting in my favor I didn't expect to topple him, like what would have happened in normal circumstances. What I did expect, thanks to his earlier lesson in momentum cancellation, was to end up in the perfect position to get a scissor lock around his head with my legs.

My legs are *very* strong.

It wasn't momentum or inertial transfer that drove Nemo to his knees and then toppled him over onto his side. No, it was the fact that his head was being squeezed like a watermelon under the landing skid of a star freighter that did it.

I could literally have popped his skull like a putrid festering boil, and there wasn't a thing in the universe he could have done about it. No amount of flailing against my legs with his badly positioned arms could save him, and he knew it. If I chose to go there, his career as a flesh-stealing wannabe immortal would be over, and he knew it.

So he did the only thing he could do in such circumstances. It must have galled him no end, but the choice as he saw it was surrender or die, and Revenants will do pretty much anything to avoid death.

He slapped his palm on the deck.

The ship's captain's quarters were, if not up to the level of opulence seen in vessels belonging to some of the Empire's richest and most self-important bigwigs, still decked-out. I suppose if one is planning on spending any significant percentage of eternity somewhere, it might as well be a fabulous somewhere.

There was a jacuzzi filled with fragrant Bornatwater that was big enough to play water-polo in and a sunken bed of evergrass big enough to host a small orgy in. The holographic walls made the place look like it was in the center of an ancient coliseum full of naked spectators, and a veritable museum's worth of priceless objets-d'art stood everywhere on diamond pedestals.

And the reason I know just how opulent it was is that the crew gave me absolutely no choice but to take up residence there. To the victor go the spoils and all that. Well, it was three and a half days flight time to the Drift and I had to sleep somewhere, so I didn't really put up too much of an argument when I was shown to it.

I wish I had, because by the time I met Jackie it was far too late to back out.

Ah, Jackie. How do I even begin to describe him? First, I should point out that calling Jackie a 'him' is not entirely accurate, for 'he' is biologically neutered. But by the time I found that out I was already used to thinking about the former captain's roommate, or pet might be more appropriate, as a male, so the idea stuck.

That he was a deliberately-created organism was patently obvious. In Her infinite diversity across the galaxy, Nature had occasionally evolved creatures that share a superficial resemblance to the human norm in a few limited features, but these are always offset by other, alien attributes so that there is never any question in any observer's mind that he is, indeed, looking at something other than human. Even on Mankind's own evolutionary homeworld, or some species share almost all the genetic code with man, no other creature can be mistaken for ourselves.

Yet Jackie, for all his differences, gave the impression of being both human and not human. His overall body plan was the same, but in almost all the particulars there were as many differences as similarities. A too-large head, too-short arms and legs on a child-size torso; all his features were human but distorted. Seeing him was like looking into a funhouse mirror that was set to its most annoying level.

I first became aware that I was not alone in the suite only after I had decided to take advantage of the whirlpool to relax my stresses away. A quick sonic shower will get you clean, sure, but it's not like it would fit my cover story to fly around with a jacuzzi on my own ship, so why not?

Why not? Oh, it was peaceful and relaxing for all of about three minutes. I had gotten undressed - after placing a couple of weapons in easy reach and posting Sam on lookout, of course - and was just getting into the feel of warm, bubbly water on tense muscles when, like an undetected meteor zooming down to ruin a peaceful wilderness camping trip, Jackie came tumbling in to burst my happy bubble.

Literally tumbling - like a court jester or circus performer. And before he had even come to a stop, perched on the rim of the tub, his lipless mouth was already up to full speed.

"Oh, yay! A new Master! How lucky can a Jackie get? Jackie *likes* Masters, oh yes!" Clap, clap, clap. "Not that Jackie didn't like Jackie's last Master, yes? But new Master can appreciate all of Jackie's skills with new eyes. Of course, Jackie's last Master sometimes watched Jackie with new eyes, oh yes. Oh, is Jackie's new Master really Jackie's old Master with a new body? Tell Jackie. Is new Master old Master? How can Jackie tell? Is old Master playing a trick on Jackie?"

"I am not," I managed to squeeze in, "either your old master or - Don't say a word! - your new master. No! I am a passenger who will only be aboard for a couple of days."

The little creature's almost-human face went through a startling range of emotions, ranging from bewilderment to frustration to shock, before settling on awestruck rapture. "Oh, goody! A new temporary Master for Jackie!" A backward cartwheel launched him off the ledge and into a madcap romp around the bathing room.

Never one to waste an opportunity when presented with one, I seized upon the no-doubt brief time his mouth was not babbling to state who I am and my expectations for the remainder of the voyage.

It didn't work.

Once he realized who I am, the rest of what I said might as well have remained among the infinity-filling volume of words unuttered for all the effect it had on Jackie.

As I dried off and dressed, all thoughts of a peaceful soak long dissipated, I tried my best to ignore the gleeful ramblings of my exuberant companion. I don't know how - or even why - Capt. Nemo put up with him, but I knew that the only way I was going to be able to complete the trip without killing the little pest was to have him kept away from me.

That Nemo's quarters were the only place I was going to be allowed to lodge was not open to debate. Being forced to share them with Jackie, though, was another matter entirely. Brexon, the ship's Number Two, had told me to call upon him if I needed anything. I had every intention of doing my utmost to avoid taking the Revenant up on his offer - as any halfway sentient being who has any desire to retain ownership of all his body parts will - but after a few minutes with Jackie I was more than ready to work a deal for his removal.

It just wasn't going to be the kind of arrangement that Revenants were used to being a part of. After all, they were usually the ones who came out on top.

"He's got to go," I told Brexon a few minutes later, having summoned him to the cabin.

The look of comprehension on the tall man's piecemeal face told me that he had no doubt as to which him I was referring. "Ah, yes, well, Jackie can indeed take some getting used to. If one does not share our enlightened taste and amusement, at any rate. Perhaps if you were not so rigid in your attitude you could begin to appreciate…"

By this point I was most definitely not in the mood to tolerate being used as a step on anyone's self-superiority ladder, and certainly not by a Revenant.

"Do not go there," I told him slowly and quietly. The same tone of voice has been known to stop a berserk Loftian telk-trader dead in her tracks, in the middle of the Czetna bazaar no less. Brexon wisely took the hint.

"Very well. I'm sure we can come to an acceptable agreement concerning Jackie's disposition."

Once a Revenant, always a Revenant.

"Agreement, nothing. I'm giving you an order and I expect you to carry it out."

"Perhaps if you were among your Imperial subjects such would be the case." He shook his head in negation. "But, alas, we are far beyond the bounds of your precious Empire, in both space and culture. You are aboard a vessel of the Eternals now, and it is our ways that you will abide by. If you wish a service performed, payment must be rendered. What have you of value to me that I would undertake to aid you in this matter?"

I'll admit that while I am seldom one to jump straight to the most drastic response to someone who takes such a disagreeable attitude with me, in this instance my first impulse was to quickly and permanently rid the universe of one particularly annoying Revenant. Saner thoughts followed rapidly on the heels of this temptation, sparing him his stolen life, yet to this day I'm still not sure I did the right thing in letting him live, for who knows how many more innocents he has gone on to maim in his selfish desire for immortality?

In any case, he still needed to learn, and in no uncertain manner, who was truly in control of the situation. Drastic times call for drastic measures.

"I thought I made it clear to your captain that I will not tolerate your usual high-handed behavior. I see now that another demonstration of my resolve is in order. Mayhap you will benefit from being on the opposite side of your flesh-thieving equation for a change." (Sam, swallow his right hand, please.)

The shock of his stolen hand being suddenly compressed down to nothing in far less than a second took a noticeable interval to register on his mind. When it did, though, the effect was quite evident. His expression of confusion about my pronouncement suddenly turned into a wide-eyed surprised followed by something he'd probably never experienced before - true, overwhelming pain.

He grasped the stump of his forearm in disbelief as a cry of pure, raw agony ripped its way from his throat. He probably would have gone on with his emoting, but I stopped him cold. The key to making a demonstration of absolute superiority such as this truly effective is, like in so many other things, in its follow-up. I had to show that I had no sympathy whatsoever for his plight, that I was morally capable of perpetrating much worse upon him should he not live up to my expectations. Ignoring his reaction entirely, I told him in the same calm, steely voice to remove Jackie from my quarters immediately.

He took the hint. Jackie was removed and I spent the remainder of the journey blessedly free of any further interaction with the Revenants and their creepy, annoying pet.

CHAPTER 11

Whenever Merkel's Drift is portrayed in popular entertainment, it is invariably shown to be a roughly-carved hollow asteroid, complete with dank, dark tunnels and dust static-clung to every surface. And admittedly, that image does fit with the near-legendary stories of its earliest days. It did indeed begin as just another rock orbiting some obscure, unknown sun.

But that was over two hundred years ago. If there is anything left of the original asteroid's material, it is well-hidden deep under all the layers of repurposed starship modules and ad-hoc growth that has sprung up between and around them over the centuries. The exterior is now a lumpy, misshapen, piebald, roughly cylindrical conglomeration of metals and ceramics some two miles long and about a quarter of that wide. To look at it you would think it nothing more than a graveyard for abandoned and obsolete hardware held together by its own gravitational attraction. Yet the most amazing aspect of it is not the fact that it is home to several hundreds of outlaws and misfits, but that the whole mashup is actually capable of starflight. The beast probably makes use of since some of the strongest structural-integrity force generators in the known galaxy, but there is no question about it being able to get around under its own power. And as complicated as maintaining such a finely-balanced system of force emitters and hyperspace nodes may be, doing so is the only thing that has kept it from being tracked down and destroyed over such a long and infamous history.

Not that mobility is it's only defense, though. Not by any means. Before we even jumped in-system, Captain Nemo had had to transmit highly-encrypted codes known only to him from three different, very specific locations. Then there were all the automated defense platforms. I've seen high-value military target star systems with fewer zip-kills floating around. If a fleet where to catch up to Merkel, it would have to be ready to run a gauntlet that would make the approach to the Imperial capitol look like an easy jog through the parklands of Sunnywald by comparison. And don't even get me started on how many different types of weapons I could see bristling out of the station itself. It looked like every single starship to visit it over the last couple of centuries had left one of its biggest, nastiest guns behind. No, no one who dropped in uninvited was long for this universe.

It's a good thing I had brought some time Revenants with me. Good for those currently aboard it, that is. Because if they had tried to use any of those defenses against me, Sam wouldn't have hesitated to swallow every last quark and erg of energy in the entire star system to protect me.

"I want you to know one thing," Captain Nemo said to me as we made our final approach to our assigned docking berth. "As high as I am among the ranks of the Eternals and as much as it pains me to acknowledge this, my status counts for very little in Merkel's eyes. Even I cannot demand an immediate audience for you. Once you leave my decks you will be on your own. Your requirement of the Order was fulfilled with your arrival here."

His haughty look of superiority had returned with his return to the bridge as if his earlier defeat had been nothing more than a momentary blip of static on an otherwise crystal clear radar screen. And since I was about to take my leave and likely to never cross paths with him again, I could have let it go.

If it had been anyone other than a Revenant I suppose I perhaps would have. I *have* been known to allow a defeated opponent to reclaim a shred of dignity at my expense. It's one of those things the nobler of us are told we are supposed to do occasionally.

But I really don't like Revenants. I don't like

what they are, I don't like their attitude, I don't like their manipulation and entrapment of anyone who is not one of them. I don't like anything about them. So no, I was not about to let that last comment stand.

"I wouldn't expect a mere delivery driver such as yourself to have any influence among the real movers and shakers in the galaxy. Of course your usefulness to me is at an end. Now stand aside while the fate of this motley little rock is determined by your betters."

What I did next I could have just as easily done without speaking aloud, letting my internal systems handle everything, but it was so much more satisfying to demonstrate the true extent of my superiority to this bunch of body-stealing miscreants. And who knows, anything that makes them think twice about messing with Imperial tech might just save some poor innocent from suffering at their stolen hands at some point in the future.

Turning to face the ship's adequate but nothing special comms console, I told it to open a channel directly to Jonah Merkel. Now, everyone aboard knew good and well that there were several reasons why such an order could not be implemented. There were so many layers of security and encryption and set-in-stone policy involved that there was just No Way that an average, run-of-the-mill newly-arrived ship could possibly ever put a call straight through to one of the most powerful outlaws in the galaxy.

So imagine their surprise when that's exactly what happened. There isn't a computer or comms network out there that can't be hacked given so-phisticated-enough software and sufficient com-puting power, and you'd better believe I packed some of the best there is. Within seconds The Man himself was visible in the 2D monitor screen atop the console.

Jonah Merkel was nothing special to look at physically. His medium length brown hair and average blended-ancestry features could have be-longed to anyone anywhere in human space, and what could be seen of his shirt was ordinary enough, a pale yellow V-neck pullover. Yet the ex-pression evident on that face was one that only someone very self-assured could pull off in such a situation. Not shock, nor surprise, nor fear.

He was smiling in amusement.

"I don't suppose there's any need to question your identity. My security systems are top-of-the-line and supposedly 100% unbreakable. For some-one to waltz in like they aren't even there tells me all I need to know. So what can I do for you, Your Highness? I don't suppose you've come all the way out here just to invite me to some charity fund-raising gala back on Alphum."

I returned his smile. It's the universal cover-up expression, capable of hiding all manner of less-savory emotional states and intentions. The time would come soon enough when he would have no doubt whatsoever as to my true feelings toward him. Until then, we both knew how to play the game. "I believe that you would prefer our business to be conducted in private... Unless you want to give my driver here something for free, that is." I couldn't help tossing in that last part. I really don't like revenants. It might be mighty unpolitic of me, but there it is.

"Oh, by all means, do come aboard. It's not like I could stop you. Not with your little friend along."

His knowing about Sam's existence didn't really surprise me. He did, after all, deal in information and he was about as top of the dung pile as they come. But for him to throw it out for Nemo and his ilk like that, well, that told me he thought he could play dirty pool with me.

Let him try. Bigger and badder than he have fallen to me. "I'm glad you understand what's at stake. This is such a fragile-looking lash-up you have here. It would be a shame if the Big Bad Wolf here were to huff or puff nearby."

Merkel's demeanor didn't change, but I was sure I could sense a drop in his cocksureness level as he said simply, "Indeed. Your guide awaits just inside the airlock," and closed the connection.

Nemo was much easier to read. Apparently not among the Ghouls who were privy to knowledge of Sam, he clearly wanted in on whatever secret Merkel and I were alluding to but knew he had no way of satisfying his curiosity. I don't think Merkel had intended his innuendo to have quite that effect, but hey, I'm a past master at turning an opponent's thrusts to my advantage. It felt good to leave the Revenant ship on that note.

There are, it seems, certain universal concepts that make themselves known wherever stay-at-homes set up places to welcome travelers into their midst. Way back at the dawn of human history, when the first nomad wandered into the first village, there were probably already a dozen shops set up specifically to liberate him of every last valuable possession he could lay claim to and replace them with cheap, unnecessary baubles he would lose all interest in the moment he walked away. And competing with these were the establishments where he could wet his whistle, dip his wick, get into a fight, or any combination thereof.

With the rigid selection criteria for admittance firmly in place, Merkel's Drift visitors were guaranteed to be in the market for some or all of these trades. Starship crews being how they are, it could not be otherwise.

Now, I am not going to try and convince anyone that I myself am always immune to the siren call of such diversions. For starters, absolutely no one who knows anything about me would ever believe it. I do, on occasion, seek out just such places and pursuits.

Okay, maybe more than just occasionally. But never have I allowed such to sway me from matters that have a great weight of importance, and very few there are that I would rate higher than my quest to rescue the innocent Melanada and bring Lumar D'Orneo to heel.

I spared the spacer concourse no more than a threat-assessing glance.

The interior parts of the station through which I was led held no more interest to me than did my guide, a nondescript bio-aug tough. My mind was drawn to the lure of the prospect of finally, finally obtaining a solid lead on how that lowest-of-the-lowlife scum D'Orneo might be tracked down.

Jonah Merkel met me in a private lounge whose decorative theme I might well have been summed up as a shrine to high-tech weaponry. Every wall, and multiple free-standing pedestals, were dedicated to displaying lethal gadgets ranging from magnified images of microscopic nanoscale implantable armaments to full suits of combat armor, with every step in between well-represented.

If he had thought to intimidate me, it failed miserably. Once Sam assured me that none of them were powered up, I dismissed the entire collection from my awareness. There would be no mind games being played here, not by anyone but me.

The owner and head honcho of the Drift rose and performed a half bow as I entered. "It is indeed a great honor to meet you, Sire, and to welcome the Empire to my modest habitat."

"Let me set one thing straight right away," I

149

told him in a voice that made monocrystal diamond seem as soft as warm butter. "I am not here to humor you. My business out here is personal, not Imperial. And you had better believe that if I judge a personal matter to be of more import than affairs of State, I will brook absolutely no interference in it from anyone, subject or not."

Merkel accepted this with cool aplomb, giving no reaction one way or another. With a gesture toward a pair of comfortable-looking padded chairs facing each other over a low table, he said, "Fair enough. Please, have a seat. Normally I would offer I guest of such renown as yourself his choice of exotic refreshments before jumping into business, but I can see that would not be appropriate here. So, what can a humble businessman such as me do for you?"

His attempt to control the conversation didn't stand a chance against my neutronium-dense determination. "I did not come all the way out here - and in the company of Ghouls, no less! - to talk *business* with you. I need certain information, and you are going to provide it."

Now that the metaphorical gloves were off, Merkel finally let a bit of his own steel show through. "I am not a subject of your Empire to be ordered around like some landless serf of ages past. My business always involves a trade. If I provide you with information valuable enough to you to justify your journey here, you are most certainly going to pay for it."

"I do not make idle threats. You know what I'm capable of. This floating junkyard can become nothing but a fading memory long before you can even begin to regret resisting me. Now, you know why I am here. *Where is he?"*

"Oh yes, I know quite a bit about you," Merkel said softly, visibly unperturbed. He was even *smiling.* "I certainly know enough to have undertaken prudent precautionary measures well ahead of your arrival. As you must know, a man in my position has ships indebted to me all across human space. Ships that will follow my instructions unreservedly."

He gazed across at me unflinchingly, meeting my eyes dead on from his presumed position of power. "It is relatively simple to lasso up a load of gravel from a planetary ring or asteroid belt with any decent force field. A little fiddling with a reactionless drive field on a ship flying close to lightspeed can toss such a load off with all that velocity. Do you really want to find out what a shotgun blast like that will do to a living planet? I have at least six ships in at least six different inhabited systems within your precious Empire that are already accelerating toward a goodly percentage of 'c'. And they will release their payloads unless I call each and every one of them off within a certain time frame. Piss me off or kill me and I won't call. Threaten me and I'll call, but you won't know until much too late if the code I give them means stop or go."

His tone, so calm and precise while he was delivering his threat, now reverted to a pleasant pitch that might have been taken for friendly under other circumstances. "So I'll ask you again. How do you wish to pay for my services? For yes, I do have a means of contacting your quarry. I, alone in this entire galaxy, can set up a meeting with him."

Damn him! He'd probably heard that I was on my way out here about three seconds after I called the Revenants. With that much lead time, *of course* he'd devised as foolproof an insurance policy as his devious mind and far-flung contacts could come up with.

It sounded like he believed he'd come up with a viable threat, too.

But gravel? Really? Time to do a little digging. Thanks to my new neuroware's quicktime function, I could both think and communicate with Sam much faster than the human norm. This handy little ability, among all my enhancements and augs, is undoubtedly the most useful no matter what situation I've ever been in. Too bad it takes such a painful toll afterward.

(What do you think? Can a load of little rocks really pose any danger to a planet? Wouldn't anything small enough to get in under a decent meteor-defense screen just burn up in atmosphere?)

((At normal velocities, yes. But when something is accelerated to close to light-speed, two important factors come into effect. First, as you well know from Lord Kittaric's advanced space combat course, it becomes increasingly hard to achieve a target lock on something that is traveling very nearly as fast as the radiations upon which such targeting systems rely. Remember, if you can see it coming it is already here.))

(Okay, I'll give you that. But so what? It's still just tiny gravel. How much damage can it do?)

((I believe you may be overlooking the effects of relativity on an object possessing mass that nears lightspeed. The key to Merkel's threat is his intention to impose true velocity on the gravel, as opposed to the pseudo-velocity that a ship traveling via conventional reactionless drive seems to attain. Recall that a drive field alters the shape of space surrounding a vessel such that it is the altered space-time itself that moves in relation to objects outside the field effect. This is why no acceleration is felt, because in reality the ship is not accelerating even though, to the outside universe, it appears to approach 'c'. And without true acceleration, relativistic effects do not come into play. So no time dilation, no reduction in length along the direction of travel, and no massive increase in mass.))

(Of course! How could I have forgotten? An object getting close to the speed of light gains more and more mass. Every little rock will be as dangerous as a miles-wide meteor, but with still just as little surface area for the air to rub against on its way down. And going that fast, even grains of sand will survive to slam all their huge mass-energy into the planet. Damn and double-damn! I *can't* let that happen.)

((Then I suggest you find a way to beat Mr. Merkel at his gambit, for I am afraid I can be of no help to you in this. If we were already physically in a single star system under such a threat, then I would most assuredly put a swift end to such a fiendish weapon. But against multiple simultaneous attacks located parsecs apart, I am afraid not.))

And that was what made Merkel's ploy so dastardly, for even with all of Sam's wonderous attributes and abilities, even he still required time to travel from star to star. Even if we knew how many such setups Merkel had arranged and at which planets they were aimed, we could never neutralize all of them before one or more entire worlds were destroyed.

Which meant I had to find a way to make Merkel call them off.

And a way to make sure he really did.

CHAPTER 12

"**T**hreaten me and I'll call, but you won't know until much too late if the code I give them means stop or go."

That one phrase that has kept ping-pong balling around in my head, but it's particular significance still eluded me.

Bip! Bop! Bip! Bop! Bi...

BONG!

And just like that, I knew how to beat him.

"You know I can't let you carry out such an outrageous act against the Empire."

"So that kind of puts you down a peg or two then, doesn't it? How does it feel to be on the receiving end of an offer you can't refuse?"

"You are aware of the Imperial policy on dealing with terrorists, aren't you?"

"A terrorist? Me? Oh no. I am simply an honest businessman who has prudently taken out a high-value insurance policy prior to engaging in negotiations with an opponent known to possess and employ extremely lethal measures indiscriminately. In my position, would you have done any different?"

Oh, how I wanted to show him just how precise and discriminating was the force I could call upon. And I probably would have, too, if not for his 'insurance'. That, however, was a policy soon to be canceled - he just didn't know it yet.

So I merely had to play for time. And while I really don't like even giving the appearance of having been outmaneuvered, I can put on a convincing act when I know I hold an unbeatable hand.

And I *always* hold the highest cards.

"I'm glad you recognize my position. Are you quite sure you want to bend me over the barrel? After all, if things do go belly-up, my indiscriminate lethality is sure to emerge."

"Ah, but here's the thing: if it comes down to it, your losses will be so many orders of magnitude above my own that I really don't think there's any meaningful comparison to be made at all. So I ask you again: do we have a deal?"

I slumped back in my seat, giving the impression of a man who has had all his options taken away from him and is left with only the bitter taste of ignominious defeat lingering in his mouth. With a sigh, I asked his terms.

A truly heartfelt smile graced his face, the look of satisfaction lighting up his eyes and radiating out in his entire manner. "My grandfather was a true genius, no one can deny. His business acumen and foresight forged quite a healthy little trading empire out here in the wilds of deep space. I'm very proud to be heir to such a lucrative legacy. I enjoy a steady profit, and have the heartwarming satisfaction of providing a much-needed haven of rest and refuge to a large number of ships and crews that, frankly, are less than welcome in the more so-called civilized sectors of the galaxy. It is my sacred duty, both to my family name and to the galactic citizens whom grandfather Tibbon established this outpost to serve, to continue to provide a safe port where like-minded entrepreneurs may meet in privacy and security, with no worries that outside bodies will attempt to interfere in their dealings or restrict their freedom of movement."

When he left a deliberate pause after delivering his speech, I obliged him by making the offer he obviously wanted of me. After all, I was just killing time anyway. Nothing I said during this phase would carry any long-term meaning.

"So you want what, some kind of official recognition and protection? A promise of non-harassment and free passage for your customers?"

He snapped his fingers. "Nailed it in one. But then again, you are known for being quick to see through to the heart of matters. I knew you wouldn't let me down."

Still acting the defeated opponent and playing for time, I sighed again and said, "And I suppose you'd accept nothing less than an all-media announcement from me promising this, just to make sure I'd honor our agreement?"

Merkle nodded his head. "Yes, I think that would work. I'm sure that between us we can come up with a statement that'll convince everyone that this is the real deal. And with you publicly proclaiming it to all and sundry, putting the honor of the Empire on the line, as it were, why, even an untrusting soul such as myself would be inclined to believe it wouldn't be rescinded just the instant you leave here."

A dramatic pause followed, one Merkel probably thought would make me believe what he said next had just occurred to him. Needless to say, I was several steps ahead of him, having foreseen his ultimate threat from the moment he'd revealed his knowledge of Sam's existence back before I ever set foot on the Drift.

"Yeah," he said, speaking to himself for my benefit. "Yeah, that could work. I'll tell you what," he directed my way, "Just to make sure you don't pull a slick one on me after all, I think I'm going to have to add another layer of protection on my side. See, I know how much you rely on nobody knowing about your little black ace. I've seen it over and over again: you going down to some distressed world and foiling the local troublemaker by pulling off some pseudo-miraculous stunt or other. And then there are all the times *he's* pulled your fat out of the fire when the bad guys thought they had all the angles covered. So it seems to me that if another public announcement were made, telling everyone your family's little secret, it would take quite a bit of wind out of your sails."

"Alright, alright," I told him. "You've made your point. But I have yet to hear what I get out of all this."

A classic used-vehicle salesman's smile showed up as he said, "Ah, yes, I'm so glad you asked. Any merchant worthy of the name knows what his customer wants even before he does. With some buyers that is not always an easy requirement to fulfill, I'll admit. But in your case, such information is all but being screamed by the very stars themselves. Oh yes, everyone who has two brain cells or equivalent to rub together knows that the real reason you are so hot to get your hands on Lord D'Orneo has nothing to do with his actions on Villalba, or even with his very public threats against your family's rule."

His smile morphed into a knowing leer as he leaned forward. "It's about the girl. It's *always* about the girl, isn't it? Lumar D'Orneo would be just another name on a very long list that you would completely ignore as not being worth your oh-so-valuable attentions otherwise. After all, why should you waste your time going after every pissed-off con man who expresses his dislike of your Empire?"

"But he had the gall to woo your latest moll away from you, and that's something a hot-blooded macho type like you just can't tolerate. I know, I know. She might have been nothing more than the latest in a long line of conquests for you, but she was *yours*, by the stars! How dare he make off with her!"

"But here's the rub: Lord Lumar D'Orneo is worth quite a lot to me as a customer, too. He has already brought a tremendous amount of business my way, and I have every reason to believe there is much, much more where that came from. So you can understand my reluctance to sell him out to you."

Here it comes. There's *always* another shoe getting ready to drop with guys like this.

Since I was just going along with this huckster's fantasy to kill time anyway, I stayed in my role as the outmaneuvered opponent trying desperately to regain a measure of control for the time being. "Okay, fine. But I will only pay if you can produce both Melanada and D'Orneo."

Merkel chuckled. "Oh, you'll pay alright, unless you want to have to reprint all that stationary that says 'The Empire of the 99 Stars' with a much smaller number. Make no mistake -" His voice dropped in pitch and came out slow and precise. "- I've got you by the short curly hairs. If you and I don't come to an agreement, I can and will allow my planet killers to go through with their missions. And not only that..."

He paused, I suppose in an attempt to inject dramatic tension into his threat. "Once it happens, just how long do you think it will take our friend D'Orneo to launch his own fleet to do the same to the rest of your precious Empire? Not very, I'd wager."

And that's a bet you'd lose, I didn't tell him. D'Orneo wants to bring down my family and rule the empire in its place, not destroy his own potential subjects and their economic base. Which just went to show that Merkel was not operating from a position of absolute knowledge.

But then again, I already knew that.

"Now, I know what you're thinking," he went on conversationally, "Even if you pay up this time, what's to stop me from making the same threat again? Or just selling my technique to someone else? Of course you are. Well, I'll tell you why: because of what you're going to pay me."

Someone sometime must have told this clown that a pause every few sentences would make whatever he had to say sound more menacing or something, because he sure seemed to use the device a lot.

I just looked at him, waiting for the punchline.

When he deemed a sufficient length of time had passed - or maybe just gave up on waiting for me to respond - he said simply, "Villalba."

And finally, with that one word, he *finally* got a true reaction out of me. My eyes opened wide as I twitched in surprise.

It actually made sense, in a twisted sort of way. Oh, there was absolutely no way I was going to give in, but I could see how he might think trading one planet for at least six others would sound acceptable to me. And his choice of which world had a sort of poetic irony to it, as well, it being the one D'Orneo himself had plundered so ruthlessly.

"I see you can appreciate my reasoning," he said with another of his patented salesman's smiles. "I am a businessman at heart. Give me such a plum prize and I'll be so busy making deals and racking up profits that I'd never do anything to jeopardize my position. D'Orneo was a fool to walk away from such a fabulous world. Give me an Imperial pardon for any possible illegal actions I may have committed up to this point, make me governor for life with absolute judicial powers over the system and I'll have so much at stake that I'll *never* risk losing it."

And you just turn the whole sector into a Haven for every crook and pirate in this arm of the galaxy. I think not.

"Don't look at me in that tone of voice, *Your Highness*. I know good and well that you can make it happen, considering the alternatives. And it's not all bad, either - I'm sure that the Imperial Tax Bureau will find ways to dig its claws into everything that goes on there, despite anything you or I could do. So just think about all that extra revenue for the Empire! Why, with all the business I'll bring, you will be hailed as a hero for engineering such a whopping economic upturn."

He stuck his hand out in the timeless manner

of salesmen everywhere. "So what do you say? Let's shake on it and go have a drink to celebrate."

Did he *really* think I was going to let him extort a whole planet away, just like that? And then reward him for doing so? Man, this guy was way off his rocker.

I really, really wanted to start feeding chunks of his precious Drift to Sam, followed by his own body parts. But if I seriously considered doing it, I could just hear a little voice in my head telling me how he'd call his goons and tell them to release their doomsday weapons. And once that happened, each world they targeted would have only minutes left to live. There would be nothing Sam or I or anyone else could do to save them. Nuevo Catalonia would most likely be the first to go. Just thinking about the millions of subjects condemned to die on that one world alone nearly made me sick.

Besides which, doing so would get me no closer to Melanada and D'Orneo.

No, I would have to keep pretending to go along with this madman's schemes for a bit longer.

I sat back and crossed my arms across my chest. "I still haven't seen D'Orneo and Melanada. Without them, you get nothing. If you want me to even consider such a drastic reordering of galactic affairs you'll have to do better than just promise to produce them at some nebulous future time."

"Oh, getting Lord D'Orneo here won't be a problem," he said with a dismissive wave. "He's been wanting to sell off some new techno-toy he came across not long ago. All I have to do is tell him a couple of potential buyers have shown up and want to bid on it and he'll come running. Now, in all honesty I can't promise you he'll have your girl with him, but once you get your hands on him I wouldn't think anything in the galaxy could keep you from finding her pronto."

That was no more than I had been expecting, but I still had to play the role I had come on stage with, if for no other reason than to see how he'd react.

"Maybe, maybe not, so no, not good enough. You'll get him here, in my hands, *with Melanada*, before I go public. I'll accept nothing less. We can allow no chance for him to learn what fate awaits him here."

His smile turned a little lopsided. "Then I guess we'll have to hope the talk I hear about him keeping her close at hand is true. Because we wouldn't want anything sour our little deal, now would we?"

"Just make your call. You know what I want."

He shook his head side-to-side slowly. "No, I don't think so. First, you have an announcement to record. When I'm satisfied that I am one press release away from Villalba's governor's mansion, then I call D'Orneo."

Now it was my turn to shake my head 'no'. "And leave you able to transmit it whenever you want? Not going to happen."

"And just what makes you think you have any say and what we do here?" he demanded with sudden steel in his voice. "Am I going to have to arrange a little demonstration of my resolve? A moon, perhaps?"

As he delivered his threat, I could all but picture it in my mind. Merkel places an ansible call that consists of a set of recognition codes and a target, and one of his hired mass-murderers makes a small course adjustment and issues an irrevocable command. A mere handful of minutes later, the airless and sparsely populated outer moon of Ulfgarth is subjected to a saturation bombardment of millions of tiny yet highly massive kinetic-kill projectiles traveling very close to the speed of light. The incredible amount of energy this imparts to the surface transforms an entire hemisphere into a hellish inferno of liquefied rock miles deep, a brightly glowing ocean of formerly solid surface washing in an indescribably horrendous tsunami of utter and complete destruction towards the far side of the moon. No structure built by man, no matter how well protected and energetically reinforced, could possibly survive such a terrible incarnation of Vulcan's wrath writ so large.

I could not let it happen. Not even once, not even to an almost lifeless minor satellite.

Not once.

Valuing my pride over such a dreadful price was inconceivable.

I held up my hands palms-out before my chest. "Okay, okay. How about this - we make the recording but inside an isolation field and I hold on to the only copy of it. We'll make the actual trade when you give me D'Orneo."

The sly grin came back. "Sure, why not? As long as you know what will happen should you refuse to hand it over when the time comes, I can go along with that."

"Now we're getting somewhere," I said, projecting a sense of profound relief. "But, you know something, I'm a horrible actor. If I'm all tense and nervous when we record the announcement, it'll show. And neither of us can afford for there to be any reason for people to doubt my sincerity, whether they be armchair analyst or Imperial psychologists. A gesture of good faith on your part beforehand would go a long way towards making me more relaxed and hopeful of a peaceful outcome, and I'm sure it would show through in my performance."

"Oh, I'm sure it would. Just what kind of 'gesture' would it take to inspire such a degree of confidence in you, I wonder?"

He'd taken the bait. Now to see just how big a fish I could reel in. "If I knew which systems you have targeted, and then was allowed to pick one and saw you have its weapon discharged into the local sun, why, I'd be so relieved that not the tiniest trace of anything suspicious would show through. What do you say?"

The twinkle in his eye told me just how much Merkel was enjoying our little back and forth. He was a true salesman at heart, and my knowledge of that was allowing me to play him like a six-armed sartorin master evokes the most haunting melodies from his macro-harp.

"Now, see, here's the thing. I know you know why I didn't tell you how many different worlds are on the line. Do you really think you can trick me into giving up such an advantage?"

"Well, it was worth a try."

"Alright, that was your one. Any more attempts to draw out anything you can use against me will cost you or Empire dearly."

Oh, how I wanted to explain the reality of his situation to him. It would be so satisfying to tell him flat out that if he actually went through with his threat and destroyed a planet, it would be the last thing he ever did.

The only problem with that was that he wouldn't be around to call off the rest of the strikes.

I *had* to get more information from him before I could act.

I thought about pushing him anyway, telling him that I didn't believe he had the gumption to really go through with bombarding a populated planet into a glowing cinder ball. If I did, though, his most likely response would be to grow progressively more irate, and if I didn't back off he wouldn't either. It was all too easy to see the

167

squad, high-gravity adapted inhabitants of Thulis being exterminated like so much frost under a chemical rocket exhaust.

Not on my watch.

"Okay, okay, you made your point." As much as it irked me to do it, I had to mollify him and soothe his over-inflated ego for just a short time more.

At least long enough for him to decide to attack another planet first.

"Good," he smiled. "Now that you know where you stand, I believe we are ready to move ahead. I'm sure you won't have any trouble projecting your sincerity as you record your announcement." he stood up and made a sweeping gesture towards the door. "After you, Your Highness."

It shouldn't have surprised me to find that he had a script prepared and waiting for me. Shouldn't have but did. And that, in itself, told me more about myself than it did about Merkel. It meant that he'd planned things out this way all along, sure. But more importantly, it meant that I had failed to see it coming.

And that, under the circumstances, was incredibly worrisome. What else might I not foresee, and what might be the consequences of such a lack?

The content of the broadcast was just as we had discussed. I pledged, by the honor of the Empire, to all his terms. There was even, I had to grudgingly respect, a clever clause in it that explains *why*. And I quote, "In response to those of you who will ask why your Empire is finally granting an entire class of subjects the recognition and protection the rest of you take for granted, I say this: Isn't it about time? The Empire of the 99 Stars was founded upon the proposition that all sentient beings deserve the opportunity to pursue inner harmony, free of any external compulsions. Therefore, I now publicly declare that this tenant shall henceforth apply to *all* within the Empire, not just some. With the creation of the Villalba Free Haven, *all* sentients are now finally free to pursue their own inner harmony in whatever fashion appeals to each individual."

Yep, he went there. When my great-X grandfather, Emperor Timothy Tiberius Tarkle the Founder, in his wisdom first laid down the outline that went on to become our Imperial Charter, he most certainly did not include those who preyed upon others by force of arms in his protection. I know it, I'm sure *you* know it, it's just plain common sense. So plain, in fact, that he saw no need to explicitly state it in his writings.

This oversight has often been referred to by historians and scholars as "3-T's Big Oops". The founder of our Empire was a brilliant and far-sighted man, but fast fortunes have been spent by proponents arguing both sides of this one issue.

The lawyers, of course, refer to it as eternal job security.

In any case, I managed to get through the recording of it without gagging, which it at one point I wasn't positive I could do.

Once I shut down the isolation field and pocketed the chip on which the video was stored, I looked Merkle in the eyes and told him flatly, "Your turn."

If his skull had been transparent crystal and his thoughts full-color, full-motion holograms projected inside it I wouldn't have been able to see what was going through his mind then any clearer.

One part of him wanted to call in his toughs and take the chip from me by force. I wish he'd gone through with that first impulse, too. It would have been fun dealing with his goons, besides giving me the excuse to go medieval on him as well.

Another, only slightly more rational part of his mind briefly contemplated having one of his doomsday ships level a planet and then demanding I air the recording to prevent the rest of his hostage world's suffering the same fate. Unfortunately, he didn't consider this as being conducive to his continued corporeal existence, so I didn't even get a hint as to which world he might have chosen.

Which was too bad, because that meant I had to keep pushing him to the very verge of committing mass murder on an almost unimaginable scale and yet be able to restrain him at the last possible moment.

"I'm waiting," I reminded Merkel, letting more

than a hint of my impatience leak into my voice. "I did my part. You don't want me to start to think you won't live up to your side of our agreement."

"Oh, I don't?" he shot back testily. "I think you are forgetting who is in control here, *Your Highness.* If I don't personally call all eight of my... Damnit! Now see what you... You'll regret..."

"Stop right there," the born and bred Prince and heir to the throne of the Empire commanded, in full Monarch mode.

Merkel stopped.

"The only reason you hold any power over me for the moment is that I believe it is just barely possible that not all of your ships can be located and neutralized in time to prevent a tragedy on a truly galactic scale. But know this: if *any* world is destroyed by your actions, you and all you and your ancestors have built here *will* cease to exist, and I will trust in the might and valor of the men and women who make up the Imperial Navy to see to the defense of the worlds of the Empire. Do I make myself clear?"

I could see that I had. Merkle swallowed nervously before he said, "Sure, sure. Don't get your tighties all in a wad. You did the right thing, deciding to work with me rather than fight the inevitable. This way we all come out ahead - me, you, and a whole economic class."

Yeah, that's what you think. "But only if you deliver D'Orneo to me."

As I prodded Merkel further, I once more heard

that little voice in my head telling me what the most likely outcome would be. Unfortunately, it only spoke in the broadest terms, but even so, I got the distinct impression that several worlds would still be destroyed if events played out along the current fate lines.

Now *why* that would be, I could only guess.

And when dealing with stakes this high, I could not afford to guess.

Why would Merkel calling D'Orneo cause everything to go haywire? More specifically, what would make Merkel carry out his threat?

Okay, there were two ways he could do it, either by failing to call off his hired killers or by actively telling them to go ahead. Obviously, if he were dead he would be unable to put a stop to what he'd set in motion, so that was the best incentive I had not to revoke his birth certificate any time soon.

That left option number two. What would prompt him to go through with it, knowing exactly what it would cost him? That was the real question.

Jonah Merkel did not strike me as being the least bit suicidal, nor was he an absent-minded fool prone to act being without thinking. If anything, he'd shown ample evidence of possessing a methodical, ordered mind that was always on the lookout for any advantage he could use to increase his profits - witness his whole current scheme.

Despite threats to the contrary, he wouldn't

jeopardize either what he has or what he was working toward. He was too possessive, too careful.

He wouldn't.

But I knew someone else who would.

Like a supernova sunrise dawning over a planet whose days are measured in minutes, I suddenly saw with ultrasharp clarity what must be going on.

D'Orneo knew I was on Merkel's Drift.

It made perfect sense once I thought about it. I had arrived in the persona of Jed the trader. But it wasn't unreasonable to think that someone might have noticed how quickly I was granted an audience with the big boss man himself, someone with the ability to contact D'Orneo.

Damn it! I was so sure I was finally closing in on my quarry that I let my impatience blind me to just how obvious I was being. I could blame no one but myself, and now the lives of everyone on eight entire worlds were in danger because of it.

If I let Merkel place a call to D'Orneo, the former governor would be so enraged at what he would rightly see as Merkel selling him out that he was liable to do anything. And a man of D'Orneo's wealth would have no problem finding a hired gun among the myriad outlaws currently hanging out on the Drift.

And if Merkel died, so would countless millions of innocent men, women and children.

"No, wait - don't call!"

"What? Huh? What do you mean, don't call? I thought you..."

"No. I have reason to believe D'Orneo knows I'm here. If you try to lure him here, he'll know you're throwing him out the airlock."

Merkel looked at me like I'd suddenly gone from sane and rational to a raving lunatic, but I didn't care. My vindication was the fact that the most likely future now did not include reports of global extinction events from multiple star systems.

"How can you... What makes you think...?" Merkel was obviously bothered by my certainty. I'd never heard him sputter so badly.

"And what do you think will happen if he believes that? I wouldn't want to be in your shoes, not with so many potential assassins about."

His nervousness was almost comical to observe. Between my calm conviction and his own suspicious nature, he was already far beyond doubting that I might be right. He was swaying side-to-side, his mouth opening only to slam shut again, and he could barely form a coherent thought.

"Oh my... but how could he... of course he would have aboard... why didn't I... ..."

He got up and started pacing across the chamber. "My guards can... no they can't, not all the time... he'll... Oh God, you've got to help me! It's all your fault for coming here. You've got to help!"

I have to admit, after what he'd just tried to do

to me and my Empire, the sight of him squirming like a Vorathian sky-eel on a gig pole brought me more than a little satisfaction. I was tempted to give the blade another twist or two, just as an agent of his karma you understand, but I've really never been one to indulge in unnecessary cruelty.

"Okay, listen. As things stand right now, D'Orneo has no idea *why* I'm here, nor does he know what you had set up. As long as he doesn't find out either one, both you and my worlds are safe."

"B... b... but you... you wouldn't! You're not like..."

"Oh, why not? To me, you are an outlander outlaw who's living large by enabling other criminals who prey upon *my* subjects, who I *am* sworn to protect. So tell me again why I shouldn't."

He was still flustered, but recovering quickly, I'll give him that. "I still have... there are my ships..."

"Yeah, about that. If you don't get on the horn *right now* and call them off, I'll make anything D'Orneo could do to you seem downright luxurious in comparison. Comprende?"

There went that nervous swallow of his again. Yep, he believed me, all right. He called all eight of his crews right then and there. He didn't like doing it, but that was just too bad.

And he liked what came next even less.

CHAPTER 13

"This is very possibly the best prounaise I've ever had," I told Ella Svensson truthfully. The dish consists of a type of near-fungus that only reaches full flavor when grown in a carefully tended, very delicate environmental balance under exacting conditions. To have it come out so perfectly poised between firmness and dissolve-at-the-slightest-touch and its flavor that elusive mixture of nuttiness and bittersweet takes a master's touch. That she had raised and prepared it herself both made me raise my already considerable evaluation of her and left me a tad bit envious of her husband, Villalba's Governor Olaf Svensson.

The leisure planet's first couple had invited me back for another dinner when I stopped by the planet to formalize my agreement with the Revenants. And unlike almost every other high-level engagement I ever attended as Prince, this was one I actually could expect to enjoy. The Svensson's were both eminently likable people, and at our level that was an extremely rare thing and to be treasured whenever found.

Governor Svensson nodded his head at my comment. "And you're not the only one who thinks so, either, Your... sorry. Edj."

They had both insisted on addressing me in full protocol, but I did gently but firmly put a stop to such nonsense.

My multi-talented wife here has won not two but now three back-to-back Maison Awards for her prounaise." He smiled lovingly at his wife before adding nonchalantly, "No one has ever done that before."

That occasioned a toast and brought about a round of compliments and modest denials, though the governor and I really meant what we were saying; she rightly deserved our praise.

It was not until near the end of the wonderfully prepared and exquisitely presented dinner that our conversation turned to my activities since my most recent departure from Villalba.

"That was marvelous, the way you maneuvered those horrid Revenants to take you to Merkel's Drift," Ella said after I'd related the early part of my adventure. "I applaud every time I hear of anyone getting something over on them. Though, to be sure, that doesn't come about very often."

"Not by a long shot," her husband agreed. "That was well done, sir. You are a man of considerable wit and uncommon intelligence, if you don't mind my saying so. The Empire is a much safer place to live for being under your protection."

All I could do was graciously accept their accolades. What they were saying was true, after all. Sometimes a man in my position can only sit back and let those around him express their gratitude, even while feeling inside like he's done nothing more than his duty to his Empire.

I eventually was able to finish telling them the facts of what transpired, but I apparently had omitted certain key elements from my recitation, as Ella oh-so-politely pointed out to me.

"I don't understand. You said you saw things happening in the future, then later you saw different, mutually-exclusive futures. If it's a state secret about you being psychic or something, I can accept that, but still, I thought the future was *the* future. If you saw different versions, how can you know which one is going to happen?"

I had to smile. This wasn't the first time I'd ever been accused of having some kind of precognitive ability, not even close. It was, however, the first time such a claim was actually true.

"As to the first part, I didn't actually say I *saw* the future - I said I heard a voice in my head *telling* me. A voice that originated here on Villalba, to be more precise."

Olaf by this point was grinning like a cat with a canary feather caught in its fur. Ella looked from me to him and back. "You know something about all this, don't you?" she accused her husband.

At my nod of permission, he said, "Remember our recent rash of people Peeking into the future?"

"Peek? But I thought you told me yourself that that could only be used here in our system."

"So I did. And knowing that limitation, I never would have thought to employ it in the manner that our clever Prince here did."

Ella gave me a look that said I had better come clean, and quick. Not being completely unversed in the wiles of the so-called fairer sex, I did.

"With your husband's help I contacted one of the many, many researchers studying the whole Peek phenomenon while they can. Remember, the source is an extradimensional creature that is stuck here against its will, and there are teams working to return it to its own continuum. Well, it occurred to me that there were bound to be any number of volunteers taking Peek while it still works. And while it's true that what they see under its influence are events occurring nearby, it struck me as reasonable to think that a user concentrating on an Empire-wide news feed would be in a perfect position to foresee the most likely major events to transpire."

"And what could be more major than the destruction of a whole swarm of planets?" Olaf amplified while I took a sip of the excellent local brandy with which we were capping our repast.

My reward was a smile that made me even more envious of Olaf. His wife was certainly a keeper, that was for sure.

"But I still don't grok the whole multiple futures bit," she said a minute later. "It either is or isn't, isn't it?"

I had to smile at her turn of phrase, among other things. "Well now, that has always been considered one of those great unprovables so popular among argument-prone philosophers. In a way, it's too bad Peek came along and settled that one once and for all."

"What do you mean?" she asked, leaning forward to refill my glass and giving me a teasing glance at her well-endowed cleavage in the process.

That's it, Edj, I told myself. *She's married and her hubby is right here with us.* I promised myself a trip to the casinos later, where perhaps I'd make the acquaintance of an unencumbered lady with whom to spend a pleasurable evening. *But stop thinking the governor's wife is coming on to you. She isn't; that's just your loneliness acting up.*

I took another sip to cover my lapse of thought. *Down boy.* "Well, now we know for sure that the future is a constantly changing web of possibilities. At any given moment, the most likely future is determined by the interplay between actions set in motion by our past choices and our intentions regarding that future. I was able to take advantage of Peek's ability to show what that ever-changing future would be by pushing Merkel to finally decide to act one way or another. When I saw - well, saw by proxy, anyway -

what would happen if I let him continue on that course and then forced him to change his mind, it altered that probable future."

"But why didn't the Peek show that outcome from the start?" Olaf wanted to know. "That's the part I don't get. Wouldn't it know you were going to step in and fiddle with Merkel's decisions?"

"I couldn't know for certain, but it seemed like a gamble worth taking that its perceptions of the likely futures would be limited to the vicinity of Villalba, just like its predictions. In other words, if someone here were to try the same thing it *would* show the alternate future, but by me acting so far away, all it saw were the largest, widest strokes of the time to come."

After a moment spent digesting that, both Svenssons began to slowly, softly clap their hands in appreciation. "Bravo, Sire. Well done," Olaf said. "A toast to your cleverness."

We drank to his toast, and then to Ella's similar one. It really was a fine brandy they had, so this was no hardship.

"And so you were able to foresee the result of his calling that monster D'Orneo, too," Olaf said shortly.

That brought forth an involuntary sigh from me. "But not nearly far enough ahead of time to be able to do anything to salvage the bigger situation."

"Don't give up," Ella consoled me. "I'm sure you'll track him down soon."

If only she weren't married...

"Of that I'm certain. So speaketh Prince Edj of the house of Tarkle."

We all drink to that, then Olaf asked, "So what's going to happen to that eel Merkel now? I can't imagine you'd let him get away with trying to blackmail *you?*"

I laughed. "Oh, he's seriously regretting ever crossing metaphorical swords with me, that's for sure." I sat back, taking a moment to silently savor the justice I had meted out to the former owner of Merkel's Drift.

"Oh? Do tell," Ella prompted, coming as close to begging as a lady of her class and station could in polite company.

"Well," I drew out slowly, teasing my audience, "I had to do something to make sure no one else can threaten to - or gods forbid, actually employ - such a devastatingly simple weapon against any world of the Empire. The solution is rather simple, if enormously expensive: every inhabited system in the Empire is being seeded with thousands of tiny sensor platforms specifically designed to detect and track objects accelerating toward or traveling at relativistic velocities. With coverage extending a light-hour or more from every potential target World, any suspicious contact can be investigated in plenty of time to avert a disaster."

Both Svenssons were smiling now. They knew Financial Warfare when they saw it.

"Cleaned him out, did you?" Olaf asked.

"And then some." I winked at both of them. "And you didn't get this from me, but you might want to acquire a fair bit of stock in Green Star Studios. I think they are going to seriously capitalize on being able to film a whole blockbuster movie series on their newest property, the former Merkel's Drift."

AFTERWORD

While writing the second episode of Edj of the Empire, I concentrated on expanding the backstory of Lumar D'Orneo while painting a more vivid backdrop of a galactic empire. Throughout, however, I first and foremost stuck with my first love, which is hard science fiction. Character and setting development are essential to any good story, but what I personally have always loved the most is the science and technology that can only reach their full maturity in a sci-fi setting. I'll admit it: I'm a fool for a good spaceship, advanced technology, and extra-dimensional shenanigans. Throw in some down-and-dirty action, some space vampires, and, of course, the hero driven to rescue his paramour, and by the time I completed writing this manuscript I was hooked. I already had plans for a short series, but certain aspects of Revenant's Omen just demanded to be expanded upon further. Thus, the book you hold in your hand (or see on your screen) is, if not the foundation of all that will come after, at least the next course of bricks that all else is built upon. Had this episode not, in the course of being written, suggested certain plot twists, the rest of the series would have turned out completely different and probably not as long.

I hope you enjoyed reading this episode as much as I enjoyed writing it.

Until next time...

BEFORE YOU GO

Thank you for reading Edj of the Empire: Revenant's Omen by Timothy Burns. We hope you enjoyed it. If you did, please leave a review on Amazon. It only takes a minute and makes a huge difference. We really appreciate it!

Joe is working hard on the next book in the series. Want to know when it's ready? Do you like free stuff, early access to new releases, deals, discounts, exclusives, and giveaways? Join our awesome mailing list today! https://www.chandra-press.com/newsletter

— The Chandra Press Team